My Bad Friend
by P G Seshagopal

Table of Contents

Chapter 1 – Qualities of a Bad Person

Akhil

What does true friendship mean? I don't believe that there is any true/false in any relationship. The circumstances and situation make people think and conclude as true or false.

I have a friend, whom all my family members saw as bad person. Why is he bad? He never consumed alcohol or tobacco. We had moved on ages from once considering those who consume alcohol as criminals. What made people to consider Abbay as a bad person?

1. Thinks on the other person's point of view
2. Full of energy and shows all his emotions. You should never show any emotion, that is our first lesson at school.
3. Hard working, never gives up.
4. Winning or losing means the same to him, only bothered about what he learnt from it.
5. He will never let anyone dominate him.
6. Does not have passion for money or power.
7. Never judges a person.

And the biggest quality of him being a bad person "*Against injustice and corruption*." Yes, that is a crime.

In an era where people are being so judgemental; would do anything for money/power; emotionless, selfish; honesty and truth are impractical, his profile is unfit for anything.

I had smooth sailing life so far and thankful for everything given by God to me. At this moment on this earth one of the happiest persons. If at all any regret, that would be my inability to change the perception about the person I admired and loved the most.

Chapter 2 – First Impression

We were about two and half years old, the first time we met.

We were in the only school in our town, to have a play school in early 90s. Since my mom left me at the school, crying and weeping, having a miserable face. Was sitting at the corner of class feeling that my mom does not like me anymore because of the arrival of my new brother and that is why she left me alone. All the kids around me were sad except for one.

Abbay was enjoying, playing with all available toys, falling, and counting 1,2,3 wrongly every time he falls on the ground. Myself and two other dejected children looked at each other. We were wondering, why this kid is laughing when he falls? Though we tried to control our curiosity, finally we gave up and joined him.

We started playing with toys and helped him in his count. The clock was nearing 01:00 PM and it is about time we should leave school for the day. Slowly went to him and desired to start a conversation. I do not remember exactly the way conversation happened or words we used. We both could speak fluently in our Mother Tongue and all conversation in this journey is approximate translations.

'Did your mom forcefully leave you alone here?' full of curiosity.

'No, I forced my mom to be here' said Abbay. The biggest surprise, eagerly question him 'What? Why?'

He took a deep breath, 'All kids in the neighbourhood went to school and I had nobody to play. It was very boring. So, tortured mom to send me to a school.'

The answer was quite reasonable, but how could he be happy for leaving Mom. 'Mom won't play with you?'

'Yes, she does. She will not play when she cooks, reads, stuffs like that. I felt boring whenever she was busy with other works. So, asked her for little brother/sister like my other friends in neighbourhood have. She said must wait for at least one year. It is very long time, asked her for school.'

I was thinking that all he wants to do is play and have fun. I too wanted the same and hence acknowledged the fact. In a confused state of mind, how can he desire for a brother/sister?

Everyone in my family loved me, cared for me and I always used to grab most of their attention. Whatever I do, they were always kind to me and explained politely about right/wrong until that little devil came. My mom's love entirely belonged to me alone. Everything changed from the moment he got into her stomach. Have enough reason to hate my always sleeping little brother.

'You actually want a brother?' scratching my head.

'Yes, of course. Do you have one?'

'Yes, he came recently. I wish mom took another year' in a depressed tone.

'You are lucky,' mixed expression of sadness and thrill.

Acknowledged him through a head nod, unable to feel lucky the way he thought. Nothing good happened to me ever since he came. My brother is yet to be ready, to play with me either. Talking about my brother was uncomfortable and hence changed back to his playing style.

'While everyone is sad, why you are falling, laughing and counting?'

'Just want to have fun. Knew if I start, all will join me. We can be playing instead of simply sitting. My dad always used to say, *"it is ok if you fall, make a practise to rise always quickly like a horse and never take time to get up like an elephant."* So was practising on getting up quickly.'

'Oh,' nodded my head again. No idea on what he was trying to say about horse and elephant.

He stretched his hand, 'my name is Abbay, from Vivekananda Street.' I stretched hands for handshake, 'my name is Akhil, from Railway Colony.'

He took his school bag, moved his arms over to take it on the shoulder. 'Akhil, it's time for me to leave, Bye!' He likes to call everyone by their name and others to greet him by his name.

In came the second biggest shock, how he can go by himself? No residential home is nearby, only couple of shops were there. He ran away a long way and turned into the main road where buses and cars are very frequent. Mom's first advice to school, never go to main road alone. Full of fear, shock, surprise, and curiosity sat with other kids who are waiting for their mom/dad.

On that entire day was thinking about only one thing, whether he will come tomorrow to school or he will vanish like my grandma. For 9 AM School, was there by 8.30 AM just to see him return.

He had a school bag on his back. He came running from the same main road turn. At last, my heart beat came down to normal and greeted him into the class.

Each day at the play school was a unique experience for me because of this friend. He will come up with new games and topics.

Even though we were at a play school, our teacher began teaching English alphabets and mathematical numbers. All kids at the play school were very brilliant, finished learning in a week. Little Genius! Every typical Indian middle-class child as soon as they say something, their parent or family members or neighbours, someone will immediately start teaching English alphabets and mathematical numbers from 1 to 100.

Miss started teaching rhymes in a rhythmic manner with some action. Based on my memory the rhyme was 'Twinkle, Twinkle Little Star.' We repeated them in chorus half-heartedly with some hand moments. Abbay will be playing, doing something with toys while repeating the rhymes, whereas we used to sit on the side bench and cautiously listen. Some of them won't even listen, simply play.

When Miss asked to tell individually, only he could tell complete rhyme in the same playing manners he did when we were listening and repeating. After that, all of us followed his approach. Our Miss taught us dancing, grabbing toys, showing pictures. The way they teach rhymes changed, because of him.

One pleasant evening on November month, went along in the company of my grandpa for his regular walk. On the way, we saw Abbay playing with a street dog. He lives in next street, much to my surprise and excitement. Full of joy, was about to introduce him to grandpa. 'You see how dirty the dog and the kid playing, touching all over it. Never do that, you will catch severe disease if you do that,' Grandpa told me. Not the precise moment to introduce Abbay to him. Grabbed his hand, told him *"Ok!"* little disappointed as we continued the walk.

The next day at school, summarized the other day to Abbay and we decided to meet every weekend at playground. Mostly, I will leave to play in the *"Sphere"* ground (*common play area near railway colony*) every weekend from 3 to 6 PM evening. Abbay will come there by 9 AM and probably will leave by 9 PM. Only lunch and evening snack he will take a break.

He is a big-time eater. At that age, he used to eat thrice of what others used to eat. As much as he ate, he will play for all those calories gained. He used to be taller, bigger, and stronger than me.

Slowly we were getting closer each passing day. One day he invited me to his home. Pleaded mom seeking permission and got her approval after a long struggle. She specified lots of dos and don'ts that I need to keep in mind. Got out of bed as early as 6AM, was extremely happy. Without troubling anybody at home, dressed up and finished my breakfast.

Around 10.00 AM went to his home. His house was smaller than mine. From entrance the house was full of great art work done by Abbay. From ceiling to door, everything had something written or painted on it. It was very colourful.

He had very few toys, but he made enough playing materials. The pressure cooker gasket became car steering, cycle pump became gear handle. A post office set up by means of bus tickets as stamps, shopping bills as money, and boiled rice as glue. Thrown away empty paper or wooden boxes became racing cars/trucks. He made swords with bunch of newspapers, that he used to practise against the pillar. It was a whole new gaming world for me.

His parents were not rich; he had very few toys to play with. He wasn't seeking his parent for new toys and presents. He made his own world of toy games such that even he never needs a company to play. He was not complaining or tantrum, he was so creative and innovative who managed to adapt and enjoy by what he had.

Thought repeatedly on how I change, adapt, and enjoy every moment as him. I just simply wanted to be as happy as him, cherishing life.

The one important thing came to my mind was how much he wanted brother/sister to enjoy and play. Though having a brother, I am not able to figure out how to play with this little kid, who can't talk and walk. Decided to try a little harder by noticing how others used to interact and what they do for the little kiddo. Slowly came closer to my brother making sounds, showing him toys, nothing really helped me to enjoy.

Next morning got a better idea. Let's invite Abbay to our home. Sure, he knows how to make Aryan (*my little brother*) laugh, then I can copy him. Went to kitchen where mom was cooking. She was a very strict mother and without her permission I can't do anything. To be honest no one in my family can do anything without her permission.

'Mom, I am going every Saturday to Abbay's home, shall we invite him to our home for a change.' I asked her very politely. She was not smiling and hence prepared myself to plea.

She gave a starring look on me, 'Ok, invite him. Both of you must behave yourself and not break anything.' Unable to hide my excitement jumped into her arms, pecked on her cheek 'Thank you, mom. Thank you very much.' She kissed on my forehead.

I thoroughly enjoyed every weekend and holidays with him. He was into my gaming world, full of toys, remote cars, and everything. Initially it was fun, after sometimes it's boring for both us. We started playing hide and seek, chain catch, running races, cricket by plastic ball and bat.

The moment arrived when he decided to play with my little brother. He was first making different sounds. My brother slowly turned his head around, looked at Abbay for a second. Abbay wanted to see him smile.

'Abbay, it's very easy to make Aryan cry and very difficult to make him smile at you. Only mom and grandpa know that trick. Dad and me always end up losing.'

'For sure you don't know how to play with kids,' he chortled. He came near to Aryan, covered his eyes with both the hands and said 'Where is Aryan? Where is Aryan?' and then suddenly moved the hands from eyes 'There he is.' Aryan jerked; I shuddered. Aryan is going to cry out load as it's his last day on earth and mother is going to come and yell at me. Luckily nothing like that happened.

Abbay, did that couple of more times and on the third time he kept his hands covered a little longer. Aryan slowly moved towards him and touched his hands. Abbay suddenly took his hand out and my little brother was laughing. From fear of getting scolding from mom, surprised and trying to believe what had just happened. Was it that easy to make him smile? Certainly not that easy for sure, irrespective of how many times he fails, my dad will still try every day something on Aryan to make him smile.

Abbay moved and jumped, making little moments - he *called it dance*, I never agreed. Then, he was singing rhymes, moving toys that make some sound towards Aryan, swiftly moving the remote-control car around him. I was still shell shock, unable to enjoy on what's happening at that moment.

To my joy, I wasn't the only person jolted. There was one more person in the room, pretended to be watching cricket match on TV, sneaking on things happening at the corner of the room, my dear dad. I turned my head towards him, gave a cheapish smile. He suddenly turned towards TV.

I realized Abbay was so natural and he never gets disappointed on failure. May be that was the only difference between me and him in trying to make Aryan laugh. I remembered the first day at play school, falling and getting up like horse. Well, I am a slow learner for sure.

Till now, I used to think and call Aryan - *little devil*. No more! Everyday enjoyed playing. All my toys belonged to him and took responsibility on watching over him, feeding him milk.

On turn of events everyone in my family spent more time with me. I felt like they are all loving me again, they cared more for me and gave equal attention. I wasn't sure whether it looked like that way at that time or something really changed the way my family treated from that day. Whatever it is, decided it was all because of my unique friend and will never ever lose his friendship. Every weekend and holidays were like heaven as described by my grandpa.

Chapter 3 – Importance of Marks

School timings changed to 9AM to 3.30 PM for LKG classes. The teachers formed a queue, sorted based on our height. Once the order is finalised, they separate into many three members group. The students sat based on their height. I sat on the middle row, whereas he got a seat on the last bench. I was extremely disappointed and ashamed of not being tall. To sit alongside Abbay, must grow tall. So, took health drinks and tried to eat more.

Can't remember each day proceeding or conversation between us. Good thing is, started to go school by myself, learnt how to cross road alone and walk on the main road in heavy traffic safely. Our LKG and UKG life went smooth without much drama as far as I remember.

Abbay was going to have a new member in his family. He was hoping for a brother or twins. From the moment Naren and Nirmal joined in our class from UKG, his obsession for identical twins was sky high.

During the summer holidays, his mom gave birth to baby girl. After few days, his mom and little sister came home. Everyone in our family went to their house for naming ceremony. They decided to go by the name Anjali. Same sentiment I guess, name starting with letter "A" His parents whispered name in her ears three times as per the ritual. Even though new born sister can barely open her eyes, he was trying his level best to cheer her, make her laugh and of course play with her in whatever manner possible.

Abbay went to his uncle's home in a village for the second half of summer holidays. Though I was playing with dad, Aryan, mom and grandpa, something was missing. One evening was little sad because mom scolded me for eating a full pack of chocolates. Dad always knew what to do with everyone in our family, when they are sad. He took me for a walk outside.

We went to newly constructed park for kids in the Railway Colony. All other kids were playing. We sat on the corner bench under shadows of towering trees.

'Missing your best friend?' dad asked me. I was looking down and didn't reply. 'You can write letters to your friend, if you know the address of his uncle's home.' During that time, letters are only mode of communication in our state. A very few people had land-line phones and we considered them as very rich.

The next moment I ran off to Abbay's home and asked his dad to give me the address of Abbay's uncle home.

I asked grandfather to write letter on behalf of me, but he insisted to write letter of my own as it will improve my writing skills. If I remember correctly, took five days to write a letter of one page. I was eagerly waiting for his reply and tortured post master of our colony thrice a day. One-day letter came. Opened it and saw something like inscription that used to be on the walls of temple. It's not a letter, a five pages book. After couple of minutes, read the first line *"Dear Akhil."*

It was impossible to read, no wonder why teachers always scold him. His handwriting on the four lines homework wasn't that bad as this letter that had no lines. Having lost the patience to read it, gave the letter to my grandfather. He tried his level best to help, but his efforts had gone in vain.

Then I took to mom, another failure. She couldn't read to the level I was able to read. Finally, dad came. Tried hard and told, 'Your friend can proudly say that *"No one in the world can do what I can do. Read my own handwriting!"'* Though we both laughed at it for a moment, then slowly I became dull.

Dad saw my face go down and gave a wonderful idea, 'Go and give this letter to Abbay's mom, she will be definitely able to read this.' I knew from my heart that dad will always figure out something.

Went running to Abbay's home and gave the letter to his mom. After couple of lines, asked her to read it slowly so that I can understand. She was reading it with ease, correcting whatever errors in the letter, properly understanding the meaning conveyed. Happily, came home and decided to write another letter. Dad came to me 'Did his mom came handy in reading the letter?'

Nodded my head and a teasing smile, 'you were wrong. There is always someone in the world, can do whatever we can do. She did read the letter without any trouble at all.'

We continued to send letters over the period of summer holiday. Summer holidays were over. We are five and half years old now. We are going to be in 1st standard. Abbay came home only on the morning of school reopening, fully charged up. I took the responsibility of taking my brother to school as he is going to join LKG. I had a great wrap up with Aryan and we are still very easy with each other.

At last, my wish came true. After two years, going to sit next to Abbay in the last bench. He was still taller and bigger than me. Now for my height, I am eligible to sit on the last desk in the class. Abbay welcomed me to sit next to him. Anyway, I was going to force out any one who will try coming in our way.

'Sitting on last bench won't be easy for you Akhil,' Abbay alarmed me.

'Why? You used to sit always on the last bench'

'That's true we will have lots of fun. But, as my dad says, *"everything has a cost, nothing comes free."'*

That was the most improbable punch line he had told me till date. Absolutely clueless on what was he trying to convey. In confusion, 'Well, you are with me, sure I can handle it,' with utter confidence.

'Remember, I did warn you.'

'Ok, I will and sure everything will be smooth and easy.'

We smiled at each other and waiting for arrival of our new class teacher. It was like striking of lighting, someone just ran into the class. All students stood up and I was in shock trying to figure out what just happened. Once revived, came to know that lighting is our new class teacher, Miss. Hemalatha Dhandapani. Though she is Mrs, we used to call in common tongue as "Miss!" She was very fast and straightway took attendance. She was daring, effortless in handling students. There will be a pin drop silence, the moment she starts to talk on the subjects.

All other teachers will try to keep us silent and gave punishments to stand on bench or kneel. She never punished any students. Where others failed, she simply succeeded in what they are trying to achieve. If someone talks when she turned towards board to write something, she will turn back and look at the students, fuming fierce face. That's it; no one in the class will dare to speak again.

Marks were not so important before that. In previous years Miss will give homework and we will write Monthly, Half – yearly and annual exams. I don't remember what kind of marks we were getting on KG classes. I think neither me nor Abbay failed in any exams and there were no ranks based on overall score of all subjects.

First time, we heard so much about marks and ranks. First, it was only teachers who were talking about it all day. Slowly and steadily students were afraid of marks and ranks. Other teachers pointed out the last bench boys and cursed us, that we all will fail or get very low marks or be the last rank holders in the class.

I wondered, what wrong we did? Yes, couple of times we stood on bench for talking. Apart from that we hadn't done any harm to any of these teachers. Everyone in the class got punishments, be it first bench or last bench at some point. Then why teachers cursed only the last bench boys? The question lasted in my mind for a very long time and even now I hadn't got the answer that can convince me that they were right.

Our examination schemes changed drastically. We now have Mid-Term, Quarterly, Half-Yearly, and Annual exams. After first mid-term examinations were over, we got the total marks and ranks. I got 96% and fourth rank, Abbay got 93% and fifth rank. One of the girls in our class "*Vasundara*" got the first rank. Safina, who got third rank, was crying that she got only 96.5% and missed first rank. She was very much afraid because her mom and dad will scold/beat her.

We were laughing at her in the last bench and Abbay invited me to come home, to show the gift that his dad bought. The moment school bell rang, we ran very fast and reached his home. Abbay, happily showed the report card to his mom and dad. Both were very proud and his dad gave the gift a small car. Abbay was so excited.

After a while, Abbay sat on his father's lap and told about Safina at school. He laughed 'You don't be afraid of me. Memorising and scoring 99% don't do any good to our life. Always learn, try to understand, that will help you in life.' From the kitchen Abbay's mom shouted, 'Your father used to get only 60%, that's why he is saying like this'. His dad whispered 'Ushhh....' kept his finger in mouth.

Their family was different, no body trying to dominate anyone. Only love and joy decorated the house, no costly furnishes or showcase or dolls or false ceiling.

I was confident that my mom and dad are going to be so proud of me, because I got three percentages more than Abbay. I was jogging and dancing along the way back to my home. Took the report card and smiled - *all teethes were visible*. Gave my report card to mom. She went through the report card for a minute, 'You need to start studying more time on weekends and less play. Have to improve your marks on Maths and English.'

It was like someone had stabbed deep into my heart. I was trying to say something, only air came out of my mouth in a complete disbelief. Mom looked dull while she talks or plays with me for the next couple of days. Though dad was very proud of me for the marks, mom's silence and distance hurt me the most.

I came to realization that marks are very important. I want my mom back the way she was. The first three years of my life, before Abbay's arrival, she was everything to me. I can't withstand her silence anymore. Pledged to get first rank on Quarterly exams and win back my mom.

Concentrated more on studies, skipped couple of weekend play days with Abbay and was serious in studying and listening class. Abbay conveyed his displeasure watching me like this and kept on reminding me, to not to become a book worm like some students in the class. At that time the only thing matter to me was getting first rank.

Vasundara and Safina always like *"Know it all, Genius!"* Though they were very popular in the class, Abbay and gang hated them. Results of Quarterly exam came and I got the first, Safina and Vasundara got second and third rank respectively. Safina was weeping for missing the first rank.

I can see my mom face glow on seeing the report card, she hugged and gave a kiss on my cheek. For what it felt, I was cent percent sure it worth everything. She told all her friends in the colony that her son got first rank in exams and was very proud of me. That moment I decided to always get first rank, keep that glow in her face. I don't remember an occasion where missed the First Rank. Only in public exams got state fourth, still got school and class first.

Next day at school, I got hero like treatment. Some of the persons in the class who barely even talked to me before were speaking with me like their best friend. My biggest surprise came when Vasundara and Safina were praising me a lot. I politely acknowledged and moved on. Back next to Abbay and smiling. There was no big fuss as he already congratulated me yesterday. It was same, nothing changed and I liked that behaviour the most.

All teachers became very fond of me, praising all the time and showing me as an example for others. Only Miss. Hemalatha, acted normally. Many teachers asked me to sit on the corner place alongside first bench boys. I was reluctant to stay next to Abbay.

One-day Vasundara complained about last bench boys about talking and teasing, especially - *Abbay*. As usual, teacher didn't hear his part and asked him to kneel till lunch. He is now familiar to it and so strong, he barely feels any pain. I know this is wrong. Vasundara was looking at him, a teasing smile and I lost my temper there. I stood up and voiced for him and all other last bench boys. Since, I am the rank holder of the class, teacher accepted my argument and warned Vasundara for false allegations. The whole class including Abbay was looking at me stunned, except Vasundara had a cruel and cunning expression.

The next day came the vital blow, the first of many incidents for my family members to hate Abbay. Aryan, Abbay and me, were playing cricket with a plastic ball on the veranda at my home. Aryan bowled a slow ball which Abbay hit ferociously. I dived like dolphin in the sea trying to catch the ball. Unfortunately, after taking the catch, fell on my mom's favourite flower pot. It fell from a good two feet height, a big crackling sound.

Mom rushed into the scene in fear. She was glaring at us and checking whether we are uninjured. She finally noticed the broken pot. She raised her eyebrows and her big eyes became further big.

Mom stared at Abbay. He got bat in his hand. 'How many times had I told you three not to play outdoor games inside?'

I ran and grabbed her hand, 'It wasn't Abbay. I broke the flower pot while trying to catch the ball.' Still thinking where I got the guts to do that.

Her face grew in anger. We can hear her teeth crackling sound trying to control, big eyes and most furious look on me. She was much scarier than Miss. Hemalatha. Everyone was silent for a moment. All three were shuddered to look at her face. We kept our head down, said in chorus 'Sorry!'

'Go, get out of here. Go out and play. No more playing inside the house. Now, don't you dare to go and play on the road, go to Sphere ground.' All three of us nodded our head and kept running right to sphere ground.

After many deep breaths, Abbay said 'I have walked alone near a grave yard at midnight in village, never ever scared of anything. I must admit that was the scary.'

'We should Thank God, she let us go, she was angry,' Aryan still had a worried face, yet to recover from the shock.

'Yap, that's right. Lesson learnt - *walking with dead people is much easier than crossing with my mom,'* concluded with a smile.

We laughed for a little while on what happened and moved on towards the corner of the playground to continue our match.

Chapter 4 – Playing with Big Boys

The academic year ended. During that summer holidays, got permission from mom to go and play in the ground by morning itself. Aryan must stay at home as it was very hot. I was at sphere ground by morning 9AM. Abbay, came after few minutes and rushed into a group of big boys.

Some of them were studying in college and Abbay was only to their waist high. They were busy in splitting the team for cricket match. They asked Abbay to stand behind the wicket keeper. Every time the ball went pass, he used to run and get it back into play. Anywhere within 400 meters' ball went, he went on chasing and the guys who were playing in the middle preserved their energy levels.

At first, I was running along with him to catch the ball. I wasn't as fit as him, after an hour decided to sit on one of the parked cycles. He was running after every ball that went to some other place other than the playing area. He grabbed it and gave his full effort in throwing them back. His throws come with four or five bounces or sometimes when he chased beyond boundary ropes it will reach them rolling on the ground.

Around 12 PM they finished the game. They gave couple of throw downs at us and asked us to bowl a few balls. I was very hungry and barely had any energy to walk back home for lunch.

'Abbay, it's too difficult in this sun to play for this long, how do you manage?'

'This is your first day playing, that's why you are feeling like this. After a couple of weeks, you will get used to it'

Almost going to faint under the tree, gathered all my strength and told him 'We were not actually playing. We were doing ball boys stuff out there. I don't think there is any good in it for us or it is going to help us improve our bowling or batting skills. We can never match their abilities. They are big, powerful and know too much about the game. Even with your strength and knowledge on cricket you can't win them. We should go back and start playing by some one of our age.'

'All fair points. I am no match to them. Only for now, soon I will be playing with them and I will score lots of runs, take lots of wickets and will be a better fielder than any of them. As my dad say, we can't build Taj Mahal in a day. It takes years to do a masterpiece like that.'

'What? Your punch lines never made any sense to me. What does Taj Mahal have anything do with cricket that we just finished? Are you going to build something by chasing, catching, and throwing the ball?'

'Punch lines and me?'

'Yap, every time when you start as dad says.... I used to get lost there.'

'Ha, ha, ha!!' he laughed ear-splitting like a movie villain.

Gave a grim face to him and said, 'You are watching too many movies nowadays.'

We went for lunch. I used to be specific on what I want to eat. Always less vegetables and mom used to force me to eat a little more. But, that day no specific omission from the food plate and was asking for more. The way I ate surprised her, but she had an unusual satisfaction.

Abbay was there before me at the ground. He was having plastic ball and bat. Now I got my smile back, ran towards him and six more of kids around our age group where there. Under the big tree, a mark about 2 feet from ground considered as stumps. Three members each in a team and only offside (*Right hand side to the tree*) scoring. Abbay hit lot of fours and sixes, took wickets at his will and obviously, we won. I always used to take his side whenever there is a team split up at place.

By 4.00 PM, ground again filled with lots of young big boys. They were playing football, cricket, badminton, and tennis. Abbay almost went to each group helping in grabbing balls outside of their reach or marking lines, etc. I lost interest in whatever he is doing out there.

After 6 PM, slowly, people started to come for walking and play begin to reduce. Abbay came and joined me under the tree. I know Abbay will give a big boring lecture and advice if start asking him how I feel about the day so far. Anyway, used to his philosophies and in some cases, I do like them.

'I don't like what you are doing out there. These big guys are simply using you. When we played with our friends, it felt good. These boys are chuckling behind us and don't have any respect for you.'

'Well, I feel a little different. They are kind to me. They won't yell or shout or scare me. If they do any such thing, from next day I will switch to other games or teams. Of course, playing with our friends was pleasant, but there was no challenge for me. From ball one I knew I am going to win, going to hit sixes and fours, how to get everyone out in an over, what's the fun in that? Out with them I am nothing, they can take my wicket easily and hit me for many runs. The ball is hard to grab, impossible to catch when it goes high. All these things present a challenge and I like it.'

'Still, you are not in their team. Only they give you an over to bat and couple of over to bowl.'

'Fair enough for me, they are at least giving that to practise something at their level. I never asked them for any of such things, they are giving by themselves. Now, let's come to the point. Do you think I am simply going behind the ball and grabbing for them?'

Straightened by back bone and sitting pose, 'U.... U... You are doing something else?'

'I am learning how to bowl, how to shine the ball, how can I swing the ball, how to hit balls that are coming to your head, how to spin the ball, different shots and diverse ways each player play. In the morning, we played with a group, I know each of the player's strengths and weakness in the game. Now can you tell me any one in that team who can throw accurately over the stumps? I will throw every occasion from any direction, it will come in one bounce or ten, but it will always reach the player near stumps without him needing to move even an inch. I observe them, practise catching and throwing as of now. One day I will impress them with bat or ball or fielding and then I will be in their team.'

'Ok, what about other sports group you help?'

'Cricket is not the only game. I like playing games and the fun in it.'

'You are not afraid of losing or humiliated?'

'Well, as my day say...' I raised my hand and told with a very serious tone, 'Stop right there. Only tell the answer to my question and I don't want to hear any more punch lines.'

Abbay chortled 'This is not a period for good advice. I am not afraid of losing, and humiliation is something that you feel about yourself, I believe it has nothing to do with others. Losing is inevitable. You must accept that fact. When you stop worrying about losing, you will be able to apply your entire skills at the task.'

'You are speaking like my grandfather. And last few minutes of this lecture was the worst boring material you have produced so far.'

He spoke like a matured man, who has seen everything in life. I was sure, it was all his dad words and preaching, as I am being at the same age.

'One day you will realize all my golden words, in fact my dad's golden words. That day you will be grateful for me. I have great trust in his words and so far, nothing went wrong for me.'

'Your father talks more stuff like this? How are you bearing and listening to them? Your dad was always jovial with us, never spoke any boring stuff.'

'Well, to be honest I don't exactly tell what my father says. Adds few bits and pieces here and there to be more dramatic and warning you, all great intellectuals are hated/boring initially and after they gone then only people realize their greatness.'

'Ha, Ha.' I was having a thundering laugh 'that was really funny!! Keep talking on your day dream, I like it.'

His face turned blue. Gave a tap on his shoulder and said, 'Let's go home.'

Though teased him, the thought on his boring speech kept me awake the whole night or may be the pain on my back and legs. He is playing better than us and beating us with ease because he is playing with bigger and tougher guys.

Next day I joined him again. 'After you heard my speech, I thought today you won't come. You made sense of much boring......ggg... lecture, right?'

Nodding my head 'To be honest, you are right. I observed only half of your lecture anyway. Whatever that matters to me, only took that part.'

'Akhil, no need to accept truth like this. You might have simply ignored it.'

Dropping and raising my shoulder as some hero did in a movie, 'I am having a stupid friend who advised me *"try always to tell the truth, even it is going hurt badly. Only lie when it makes life better for someone or avoids hurting many people."* Just trying to follow his stupid idea.'

Abbay had a bright pleasant smile 'You are making me proud, Akhil!!'

'You know that idiot is very confusing about everything. Sometimes he tells *"not to be proud of any of your own accomplished"* and on the next second he says, *"I am proud of myself."* Very difficult to understand.'

We both stared at each other for a moment with a cheapish smile. Abbay slowly whispered, 'You know what my dad used to say..........' I just took off right into the playground to catch the ball without any intention to look back. Abbay was shouting, 'You know, it hurts!!'

Chapter 5 – Enemy to Friend

We played on each day of summer holidays. As I estimated before, mom asked me to go only in the evening as it is getting very hot in the noon. Like the previous year, Abbay went to his uncle's home again. We communicated by letters for the whole month. One improvement, I could read them myself. May be his handwriting got good or I became an expert in reading those scribbles.

Beginning of another year at school and we got our usual last bench. Everything was new: new teachers, new benches, new black board, and new punishments for last bench boys. The severity of punishment varies based on what we do, mostly for speaking during class hours, circling our ground ten rounds is the punishment. If we have pending homework, then we should stand up on the bench or kneel for half a day. Not exactly half a day, for a little longer period than it was in the previous years.

We had only three hours a week for sports, that too our sports master will make us do same old boring exercises. Abbay hated the idea. As soon as this punishment introduced, he was very enthusiastic. As long as the teacher is telling delightful story or something interesting, he will listen attentively. Else he will start talking intentionally and gets punishment.

Many in the class were afraid of this new idea of punishment. Some of them even fainted in severe Sun. Teachers scared us telling how other students had fallen unconscious and how difficult to walk the next day. It wasn't a great deal for the last bench boys. Some of us were fat, but they managed to survive.

Vasundara became class leader and everyday one way or another she will get Abbay's name on the list of students talked when teachers were in the class or in their absence.

After couple of weeks Abbay got furious and started teasing Safina and Vasundara. He kept pet names for them and called them, mocking like calling one of his friends. One such day during sports hour, Abbay mocked Safina, the way she talked, walked, and whipping for silly things. He was projecting how selfish and cruel she is. Everyone in the class including our sports master enjoyed the show. She was so humiliated that she complained about him to the headmaster.

Our HM came into the class. He is close to 7 feet tall and had a big belly. He is having a wooden stick in his hand. Everyone looked frightened. He shouted at Abbay for his mischief. Took him outside to play ground area, we all tried to sneak and see what kind of punishment he is going to give.

I was afraid HM will beat on his thigh and back. Abbay may not be able to walk and go to restroom properly for the next couple of days at least. Will he end up in hospital or will he bleed and get a syringe? All sorts of non-senses came to my mind.

Our HM was very good man and he always spoke softly to everyone. He looked around to check whether anybody is watching. We are hiding against the big wall.

'They told you are very good at mocking, show me what you got,' HM with serious and cold voice.

Abbay looked at him and instigated mocking Safina which he considered his best performance till date. Yes, it was. HM guffawed and so did everyone who was watching from behind the pillar. We were having a blast for the second time within a day! HM clapped and asked Abbay to stop. 'You are good, really good at this!! Now in my school days I was also good. So, let me put a show for you.'

We are all on the edge of the platform road about to fall. He mocked himself initially and then slowly he mocked Abbay's mannerism. It was so funny and Abbay clapped and laughed. But slowly his happiness faded and his face became sad. He kept his head down.

HM stopped his play 'Sorry for hurting you badly. But I had to do this to make you realize, when you are making fun of others, how much it hurts.' Abbay with tears in his eyes 'I was just trying to make others laugh with my body language and expression. My intention was not to hurt Safina or humiliate her.'

HM put down his hands on Abbay's shoulder 'It is a great that you want to make people laugh and you have a very rare gift to actually do it. There are many ways to make people laugh by telling jokes or doing other things. Mocking the way someone behaves and shows emotions is inexcusable.'

'I am unaware of jokes or any other things. Mocking somebody just comes naturally.'

'You have all signs of a great actor and you will do wonderfully well with drama. But, if you are mocking a person, one way or another you will end up in hurting his/her ego and self-esteem. Real comedy is hurting yourself with body language and expression to make others laugh on you, not by hurting one person and pleasing other, understood?'

Till date I was thinking Abbay was the most boring philosopher and lecturer giving advice about good, closely followed by my grandfather, among people I have ever come across. After this act, I changed that thought.

'I am sorry, Sir. I will ask her to forgive me and I will never hurt one to make others laugh, except for myself, and I will participate in drama during this annual year celebrations.'

'Good. You are smart one. But I must give some severe punishment to make her happy and avoid others doing any such things in future. Now you tell me what should I do?'

Abbay was extremely clever and knows exactly his strengths. 'Give me 50 rounds circling around the ground'

'Sure, you can do that? 10th Standard students will be unconscious by 25 rounds. If you faint or get severely hurt, you should convince your parents.'

'Don't worry, Sir. I promise you, there won't be any trouble. I was thinking of 100 rounds, 50 is piece of cake. Just now had my lunch also, I am absolutely positive.'

He dragged him to the centre of the ground. He screamed at Abbay 'Do 50 rounds, if you got out of breath and incomplete, tomorrow you will continue again'

Abbay used to finish 10 rounds in maximum 10 minutes. So, he was thinking HM is too kind to give severe punishment. He completed 50 rounds with continues one hour running. Though our class teachers were afraid, forcing him to go slow and gave water every 15 minutes.

Abbay was laughing and cherishing the so called *"Punishment!"* After all those rounds without a small bend of his back, walked straight cross to the class room and went near Safina, 'I have done a terrible thing and I will never ever tease or hurt you or anyone else. Sorry and please forgive me.' She was looking at somewhere else, ignoring him. After a minute, he came smiling to our place.

We were all very disappointed at Abbay for asking sorry to our prime enemy. But we over heard what HM was explaining to him. So, we tried our level best to keep it normal. As usual quarterly exams mark came and we became heroes from blood sucking villains.

Safina and Vasundara gang of people and couple of first bench boys alone hated us. Abbay is not teasing them anymore and restricting others to do the same by his big lectures and punch lines. The moment he tries to start anything inscrutable, we changed the subject abruptly or moved out of there.

Every year ever since our 1st standard, we *"The Last Bench Boys"* will get scolding, punishments, and curses from teachers till Quarterly exam. Then couple of us who got good marks will become hero or at least treated better. This myth followed till the end of my college days. I tried hard many times disagreeing about what Abbay told on teachers treating students partially based on where they sit. But the truth is, he is always right.

Rehearsals of various dramas for annual day function happened daily. Abbay and Vasundara were in the same court scene drama. Forgot what the act was about.

Abbay kept distance from her, she kept on trying to undermine him. His patience had its limits and then slowly he began to dominate. Every play and on every rehearsal, he got claps. Whenever she tried to tease him or start a fight, he acted accordingly to cut it at the root. Another rare gift he possessed.

On each passing day, Vasundara ears were burning and she found it hard to resist, everyone praising him. She sorted Safina's help and couple of times Safina tried to argue with Abbay. He was too clever to fall into their trap. Both girls together planned to humiliate him in front of all the audience during the drama on annual day celebrations.

We came to know about this and warned Abbay. He was taking them easy. He was thinking they are incapable of doing anything serious to him. The annual day came. The show is about start around 5 PM and will go up to 8 PM.

We came to school around 2 PM for his final rehearsal and make up. My eyes and ears are dialled to eleven and very curiously listening and watching everything happening around to ensure Abbay goes unhurt by our enemies.

He maintained his cool all along. The show started at the scheduled time and all parents were present in the ground in front of big stage. Safina and

Vasundara performed classical dancing that they were learning and it was good. Probably got the biggest applauds, I guess.

Half an hour before the start of Abbay's drama in which he is going to be lawyer, his over coat disappeared. Our boys are so sure it was two evil girls for sure. Staffs had less time to start an investigation as the show is about to start.

Abbay was cool as a cucumber and listening to local folk song. Only ten minutes was there, one of the students from 10th standard came wearing a black shirt. They acted as protesters and Abbay simply borrowed his dress and made tie out of a paper. 'It still doesn't look like over coat and you don't look like a lawyer' in a depressed tone I told him.

'No one will look or think about my coat, they will enjoy my act' little over confidently. As usual it ended up the same way he had predicted. He gave away a stunning intro speech to himself about his dressing and the whole crowd gave thundering applauds. Gees! What a start was that.

Vasundara unfortunately got sick and vomited couple of times after the dance performance. She was lagging and her performance was below par compared to her rehearsals.

She acted as one of the witnesses and Abbay was asking questions. She suddenly froze and unable to speak. Abbay handled the situation brilliantly by sending jokes, out of the drama script and encouraged Vasundara to perform. She suddenly got her breath back and delivered a stunning performance.

Truly it is the best so far on that night. Everyone applauded including Aryan. I yelled at him not to clap and told him Vasundara is an evil devil who catches little boys in the night and eat them. None in our gang like what Abbay did to help Vasundara.

'Why on earth, you helped?' in chorus we screamed at Abbay.

'If I let that moment, then our drama might become the worst program of this night. Everything we worked for in the last two months will be for nothing. Besides, as a team member and co-actor it is my duty to help anyone.'

'She is the one who stole your coat and wanted to stop you from acting.' I yelled at him.

'Nobody knows who stole it. Anyway, who ever done that, gave me terrific opportunity to express myself with my own script about my dress. I should thank that person. You guys know what my dad used to say....' he looked at us hoping we will stop him, but we let him continue. He said, 'Think positive, only good will happen to us.'

Fumes were coming from our ears. Vasundara got the overall young performer award and we felt very awkward. Everyone was leaving home.

Suddenly Vasundara came near us and told Abbay 'Thank you for helping me out there.' Abbay gave a wired expression and smile, my vocabulary is insufficient to describe about it. I looked at him very confused. He turned towards me, realised and then told Vasundara 'You are always welcome.'

'Sorry Abbay, for all the dreadful things that I have done to you. Let us forget all of them and be good friends forever' she stretched her hand. Without a second thought Abbay shook her hands immediately.

He glanced at me and I was shaking my head all over. After a couple of minutes, she was showing "*ta-ta*" with her hands. With all teeth out, creepiest smile, he was saying bye. I gave a big slap on his shoulder 'You fool. She is our biggest enemy and might be planning something big to hurt you very badly. It's all a fake!!' yelled at him with disbelief on what is happening out there.

'You are treating her like some movie villain. She is just a little kid like us and she realized her mistake. Don't be too judgemental. We are all going to be very good friends, you will see.'

'You had gone mad. Hope tomorrow you will come back to normality' I ran towards my dad's motorcycle.

Chapter 6 – First Fight

From next day, school turned upside down. There were many gossips on Safina and Vasundara split up. Vasundara shifted her place to last bench of girl's row, only little away from Abbay. She was talking frequently with him. She came to break with us and shared lunch with our gang. Day by day she was getting closer to him. I was still having a fussy feeling about her being friends with us. Always suspected she is going to do something unforgettable to us.

Annual exam went by and summer holidays came. When we were going on the way to home, Vasundara caught us in her fancy three-wheeler cycle.

'Hey Abbay and Akhil, what are you guys going to do on this summer holidays?'

'Will play every day at ground in April month and during May month will go to my uncle's village.' Abbay replied kicking one of the stones on ground to big garbage bin at the end of the street.

'I will be playing with Abbay and Aryan mostly' grunted.

'Great!! I am going learn the next stage in Bharatanatyam dance' Vasundara cheerfully.

'Did you and Safina patch up?' Abbay asked eagerly.

I stopped and looked at him with one of my eyebrows going up, a modern style which I like very much. They too stopped and understood the meaning of my expression. She continued, "No, Abbay. She is like that only. Leave her!'

'I got permission to have ice cream on the way to home. Do you guys join with me?' she requested politely and wanted at least Abbay to give her company.

'My mom will scold me a lot and will have a grim face for at least couple of days,' in completely depressed tone suggesting to both that I really want to have ice cream, but mom stands between my desire.

'I am good. I will join you,' Abbay said it very cool.

'Ok, you guys go without me.' I tried to move out.

'We will go all together one day when you got permission from your mom.' The moment she told it, I liked her. Instead of showing it, turned my head towards Abbay and looked upon him from head to toe nodding the head slowly. He understood my reaction and kept quiet.

The pet name Abbay gave for Vasundara is FM: *FM radio*. She is very talk-active person and will keep on talking without noticing whether you get irritated or bored or lost interested unless you switch off and move on to something else.

Same was happening and she was talking with Abbay. To my great surprise he was listening to all these and asking question sometimes. I was getting jealous seeing him and Vasundara becoming very close. She was not bad as I was thinking and know that Abbay will move close only if they are trust worthy.

Holidays started and we were spending the full day at the ground. My batting and fielding had improved drastically. My performance improved so much that nowadays Abbay is playing the entire day cricket with me. My batting was pretty good and he kept on bowling at me to improve his skills. My bowling lacked the pace and he was tearing me apart.

Sphere ground usually belonged to railway colony and nearby residents, mostly outsiders are unwelcomed here. But, on one Sunday outsiders came to play cricket in our ground. We were standing behind the wicket keeper as usual. We rarely got balls towards us. During innings break railway colony cricket team captain – *popularly called as 'Brother Sekhar'* by us, warned to be cautious of those new boys as we are little kids.

By Afternoon, the ground was full empty, only we two were playing under the narrow shadow of big tree. Abbay slowly whispered 'Do you still think Vasu stole my coat on annual day?'

It was very strange the way he told her name, 'Ohh.... she became Vasu for you now?'

Suddenly Abbay got angry and in a ruff tone 'Just a short form of her full name, impossible to short Akhil, right?' making clear that he was unhappy the way I replied.

'Ok, Ok... I don't think she stole it. She is nice at times, does have helping tendency and not a head weight Queen as we thought of her'

Abbay smiled 'isn't she? I asked her, whether she stole the coat?'

'You what? Are you crazy? The question might have hurt her. Did she cry? No, no... Did she scream?'

'She cried and requested to trust her. She is a very soft girl without any cruel intention. Then I consoled her and explained why I must ask that question. She understood and became my second-best friend.'

It's unimportant to me whether she was the thief, only the last part of the sentence mattered to me. I was very happy inside and heart beat was rising heavily. Taking the ball in hand and moving backwards chuckling. With huge anticipation and curiosity was about to ask him 'who is the ...'

Suddenly realized I had landed on someone foot. Slowly turned back to see four guys, the outsiders who came to play in the morning. Everything changed and became dark. Like a cow tapped on back by a wooden rod, whistle passed behind Abbay.

Abbay was very easy and remained super cool. Gave one of the cutest smiles to them, even a hard-hearted goon would become soft by now.

One of them said, 'You two guys will only grab ball for Sekhar? Why we are low born to have your services?'

Couple of vulgar words came by. Abbay never liked anyone speaking vulgar words. At that time the biggest bad word he knew was *stupid!* so he was still smiling at them and graciously said 'We used to help them when ball goes behind the wicket keeper. They never forced us to grab ball and brother Sekhar always asked gently.'

They moved forward and came closer, 'are you trying to say that we forced you, scolded, yelled, spoke dreadful things about your family and kicked you at your back?'

We both realized the trouble. I seized Abbay's hand. He was still smiling and in a husky voice, 'sorry brother, if anything I told hurt you. My intention was never to hurt you, please forgive us.' As soon as he finished the sentence, we ran for our life.

As Abbay was behind me, they caught him with brute force and he feel down. He shouted to me, 'Get Sekhar brother for help.' Immediately I ran towards Sekhar brother's house. The other tried to move ahead and catch me. Abbay steadied himself and gave a mighty blow on the penis of the guy who grabbed him.

Though he was twice our height screamed out load in agony, 'Mummyyy......' I stopped and turned back thinking it was Abbay's scream and was relieved to be wrong.

Abbay was staring at them with small eyes and pencil eyebrows angrily. If you are in front, you would have definitely laughed at it. Two of the boys laughed out loud.

Abbay got more furious and gave another big kick to the same person on the same place. Now he screamed so big that everyone in railway colony might have heard it.

I stopped there stone stilled in a complete disbelief. Now the other two got serious and the third guy said in fear 'let's leave, everyone heard him and they will be here any minute.'

One big 7-foot-tall guy thunderously said, 'You scared of a little kid? You should wear girls dress from tomorrow. We learnt karate for nothing.'

Soon as he finished the sentence, he moved swiftly to Abbay right and then shifted his direction completely, moved left. Abbay was firm in his position trusting his strength and muscles. But, got a big punch on the face and the other guy kicked him in the belly.

Abbay fell and I was thinking about running again. He was unaware of what just happened, but both the guys moved so fast trading blows on his ribs and face. After couple of punches, they heard couple of guys coming from the home near ground. Third guy yelled 'they are coming, we leave now.'

That gap was enough for Abbay and he is not going to quit or accept defeat. He moved slowly closer to the seven-foot guy and mounted full force, struck by his shoulder on his leg. The brutality of Abbay was so fierce that the big fell right on his face on ground. Abbay grabbed his left leg and trying to twist, while the one from behind kicked in his back, Abbay fell across. The big guy's leg bent as Abbay was holding it tightly.

I could hear a crackling sound. When Abbay rolled over him and got up, I could see tall person's broken bone and he was crying in shear pain.

By the time Abbay got up, after bearing all agony and pain in between his legs, the fat one was slowly getting up and was right in front of Abbay. Abbay gave another thunderous blow with all his strength on the same point. This time the pain was at such a level he couldn't open his mouth.

Two persons down, one standing away at a fair distance with full of fear and the other in complete shock on seeing his buddy's broken leg, it was so thrilling for me to watch and slowly moved towards them in confident.

The final one guy standing before Abbay wanted to take revenge and moved like a butterfly. Not sure what happened from a distance, the butterfly guy was crying in pain and Abbay spitted something out of his mouth and fell on the ground. The other person is holding his ears. Abbay got up, a big booming kick on his back, he went straight towards the tree, his head struck and he was bleeding.

The fourth guy in fear ran for his life to escape from Abbay, no more worried about the people coming towards them. To my surprise Abbay limbed and came right towards me, grabbed my hands, and started to run. Sekhar came right towards us and lifted Abbay like a little cub. Abbay had a grim face and they gave first aid to his wounds.

Ambulance came to pick up the remaining three guys. I was two hundred percent sure that they will have a great deal of difficulty in using the rest room for at least next couple of days.

Everyone was talking about Abbay's act of bravery and boldness. He became overnight sensation (*honestly overnight star hero*). Every house and every street surrounding the ground gossiped about it for the next week. The story magnified to such a scale that he got the status of a little don and four guys fell 100 metres away after he punched them.

They were all praise for him as a seven-year-old boy took on three martial arts students over 15 years old, not only lived to tell the tale but beat three of them in such way that they were motionless, required hospital admission and the seven-year-old boy simply walked.

Only Abbay's parents looked worried and his mom prayed a lot in temple for his healing. I felt it was little escalated, but know moms are like that only and that's why we love them the most.

Abbay walked briskly and running, playing in his usual ways. We never talk about it as he was feeling uncomfortable to recall. I felt bugging is unhealthy. But that scene is still in my heart just like it happened hours before.

After hearing this tale, there were three people worried - *my family members*. My dad went one step ahead, directly warned me and cautioned me to keep little distance from Abbay. Mom somehow knew that's highly unlikely to happen, hence she simply asked me to stay away from any fight and bad people.

Chapter 7 – Need to Learn Fighting

Couple of weeks passed by and rumours/gossips steadily settled down. One-day rain came heavily in the middle of the match and everyone ducked under tree. Sekhar was sitting beside Abbay. I was next to him.

Abbay said, 'what was it, the way those two guys used, and how they beat me?'

Sekhar was unsure on what exactly Abbay is trying to ask 'As far as I can remember you beat them so badly; they went to hospital and you only had scratches. They beat you?'

'Frankly speaking, the two boys were all over me. I believe we both had the same amount of strength....'

Sekhar interrupted and chortled, 'ohh... Really, you are equal in strength?'

'Well, I would say almost!! Because they were unable to bear my hits and only because they moved differently and were able to hit me in such a way that will cause severe pain, I got stranded.'

'If anyone hits you anywhere it will be painful only, Abbay. The truth is that day you are extremely luckily to survive and injure them. They might have dropped the guard or something like that, else you would have broken bones and spend months in hospital for recovery.' Sekhar explained as graciously as he always does.

'I totally agree. They were all over me and I was losing the fight.' Sekhar turned towards him chuckling, 'losing the fight?' Abbay continued 'Yes, almost lost it. My eyes had a problem and everything was blank and dark for a moment. Then something pumped inside my body and I got strength exactly to bring him down. The last guy fighting got my hands behind and was trying to choke. It was impossible to get out of it, luckily his ear came near to my mouth.'

'Ha, Ha' we were laughing out loud including Abbay.

'Yes, I was extremely lucky that day. I managed. The point I am trying to make is I need to learn fighting skills and their styles. Only then I will be able to defend myself in future against guys like them or more powerful.'

'Fact' Sekhar nodded his head. Sekhar was six and half feet tall, training himself to join in police service. It was his childhood dream. He knows many arts of fighting and does regularly practise them. In fact, he won many district level boxing championships.

'They were karate students, practising for more than 5 years I think.'

'I want to learn karate' Abbay eagerly stood up.

'Ok, get permission from your parents and then I will take you to the master for training. Have in mind, it won't be easy like running 10 rounds in school ground.'

'Then I will like more, I like it when it's challenging' sheer confident Abbay.

He got permission from his parents to go for karate. Every day morning and evening he spent one hour in practising. After couple of days, he got sore hands and legs. He was feeling great degree of discomfort. He always hid his pain and tried to show he is enjoying practise sessions. Our time at Sphere ground reduced drastically.

The way he was describing about karate, prompted me to taking the classes. At home, I was describing about health benefits and advantages of learning karate. My dad was completely against the idea of fighting and mom is anyway going to reject my proposal.

Abbay stayed at home itself concentrating on learning faster. He cut off his usual visit to uncle's home. Summer holidays are going to be over and school will reopen shortly. It was intolerable to ignore or dislike the way he describes on fighting. There was less about fighting and much about learning as it was a great art work.

Being highly impressed by his orchestration, requested to start teaching me during the evening play. Abbay happily agreed and we begin to train. By the time, I felt all my energy has soaked up, he will say *that was a good warm up session.* I was in absolute disarray. After few weeks bearing body pain, I could match Abbay at least in the warm ups.

Abbay's little sister came with us to school on the opening day. Anjali used to play only with Abbay and till then she will be always at home. She was very shy and afraid a lot about the outside world. In every manner, she was a complete opposite of Abbay. She disliked the idea of going to school like many other kids.

She was holding Abbay's hand tightly till we reached school. She broke out with huge noise and cried a lot while he was trying to leave her at class. The KG class teachers were kind and trying to calm her down at their level best. Anjali was too stubborn to leave him behind.

Abbay understood the scenario and decided to stay out in KG class for the complete day. He was and is very caring, protective, and lovable brother. For him she means the most important person as literally as mom. Abbay was the only world she knew till date. At last, he convinced Anjali to get into the class room.

He was standing outside her class. He knew she will cry again if he leaves her side. As he expected, Anjali turned around to check whether he was there every 5 minutes. She will give away one of the cutest of smile and turn back again to the teacher.

I was wondering this is too much. My brother too came to school on the first day, there was no fuss about it. Abbay had to lose the entire day class because of her and I felt bad about it. Got a seat on the last bench and reserved one right next to me for Abbay.

Anjali was seeking Abbay to come with her even for small bathroom break. She was forcing Abbay to come into the rest room with her. The creepiness of the situation was so bad for him, as he finally convinced her for half an hour to go with Vasundara. I was beginning to get irritated. But then, I was pretty sure that he knew exactly what was happening and how to deal with it.

Our conversations were shrinking each passing day. Too many factors and forces were reason for that, Anjali, Vasundara and his daily practise. Our weekend time also got lesser because piling home works. At that moment I was thinking 3rd standard is the toughest.

Things were changing very fast. I gave lots of attention on studies as ranking mattered most for me. We used to go to sports hours, but it was for fun and joy. Before now there was running races and few more stuffs in which coming first counted, but never a serious competition.

Chapter 8 – Competitions

Our sports master used a have a digital timer in his hand and without great deal of insights he was training us for various competitions. Anything physical was bread and butter for Abbay. Only Naren could challenge him 100 and 200 metres running. On all other athletic events, you will find only Abbay on the top of the charts.

So far sports day is where we will get free cool drinks and chocolates. Not anymore. We had a bunch of participants and I stayed away from most of the events. I know Abbay is going to win everything and there is no point in trying to compete with him. I feared of humiliation by him in front of a huge crowd.

His advises or philosophises about winning and losing mattered for me at playground. Here with thousands of people watching and I can only think of humiliation when he beats me with a big margin.

Abbay forced me to participate in few events, I was unenthusiastic about it. There were few sports for kids that Abbay considered as silly. I made sure my name was in the participants list on those games.

Abbay had a brisk start winning both 100 and 200 meters' sprint. He had a good challenge with Naren, who was a close second. Naren was very thin and extremely flexible. He was quick, but Abbay ruled the yard.

Abbay ran in 400 metres for 3rd standard boys. He should be running with 15-year-old boys, running alongside seven-year-old boys is a joke. Abbay still was running like a sprint race over all 400 metres. Naren almost exhausted by first two races, gave up around 300 metres as Abbay almost close to the finish line.

With two steps away from finish line, he stood there and turned back to check anyone is nearby. The huge crowd erupted, screaming and whistling. He was clueless what just happened. He crossed the finish line and acknowledged. Though it was unintentional, by standing and turning around close to end line, he looked like mass hero. I was embarrassed and extremely angry at him for doing that.

Nobody in our age group had the guts to participate in 800 metres with this big giant. On a stunning move, our sports master put him to compete with big boys aged above 10. Abbay was relieved. Finally, he is going to have a good challenge.

He was extremely disappointed when all co-participants were running very slowly initially. He sprinted the first 200 metres and then slowed up so that the group will come around him.

They all thought Abbay lost so much energy sprinting initially and they can race him to the last 100 meters. Naren was disappointed and complaining how silly was Abbay. I was hundred percent confident that Abbay going to make it with ease. The Sphere ground was twice or thrice bigger than this and every day as warm up he will run around at same pace from the start to finish. No way on earth he is going to lose this one.

Around 700 many raised their speed and couple of big guys sprinted the last 100 meters, only to see the little boy laughing at them on the finish line. There was no whistle or scream now, a stun silence. Many of our last bench friends were in total disbelief.

He nearly won all athletics events. A complete dominant performance made him eligible for couple of scholarships and the school thought about a long-time process of moving him towards district level tournaments. He had the slightest idea of what's happening around him and hence accepted the offer. At home, he had a big welcome from his family members.

Next day at the class Nirmal was so proud of his identical twin brother, coming second and giving a close competition to unbeatable Abbay. The last bench boys got all the awards in sports day.

Naren was quiet and seriously thinking about something. Abbay greeted like a super star, but he was still the same and acknowledged in the same manner.

'Abbay, how you are able to run that fast for that long? Are you taking anything special like golden-flower or something?' Naren was expecting the reply so badly.

'It's called stamina. At karate class learnt how to be quick and last long. The idea of running long time is not to push extreme point where you will lose your breath. Always make sure you are breathing. Before karate I had stamina, but lacked speed for quick sprints. Now, I can feel my legs are much stronger than before and can stretch it for long time without going out of breath.' Abbay gave away the whole scheme.

More confusion for Naren and the answer gave him plenty of questions to clarify. 'So, no special food and special medicine?'

'No. Nothing at all. Just practise harder and harder. After some time, you will know how to hold your breath.' Abbay replied.

'On 800 metre you ran very fast at the beginning. You should be out of breath' Naren curiously.

'He was out of breath, that's why he slowed after 400 metres and almost walking for next 100 metres. Then, he went on with constant pace holding his breath.' I explained what exactly happened.

Abbay nodded his head "correct!'

Naren surprised by my comment. 'So, you are not creating scene and showing off how heroic you are?'

The question itself was very odd for Abbay. 'What? What you are talking about? Is that what you think of me? You think I am show off? You think I am that cheap?' Slowly raised his voice in anger and frustration. Abbay disliked when people close to him start to have wrong perception about him.

I understood the scenario and made Abbay realize the truth. 'Well, he is not only the one. Each and everyone in the school think the same way. Except me of course, they didn't know you that well I think,' turned around him and gave away a teasing smile.

Abbay looked at everyone in the class wondering why they are thinking like that. He was very upset that all think this way.

'Vasu, do you think I was creating scene on sports day?' anxiously questioned his second-best friend.

She was on the middle of chat with her friends and without understanding the context of Abbay's question, she replied 'Yes and you have all the right to do so. You won everything.'

That answer was a stellar blow for Abbay. He was disappointed and sad.

'So, Sir will accept only from second best friend?' I teased him with a little jealous.

Naren quickly came into the picture, 'From your point of view, karate gave you the strength to go this distance. I too will join you from tomorrow.'

Now my heart broke. Abbay convinced everyone in our little last bench boys' group to join karate except these two. He begun to give away his highly impressive speech about karate and work out to him. Change of emotion and expression, 'That's great. I will explain the importance and advantages of it....'

I closed his mouth with a hand. 'Stop, right there. He might have heard around about 1000 times about it at various angles from you. No need to explain and tell that boring, depressing lecture again.'

Naren felt relieved, I did that. He suddenly looking down at book and acted like reading something. Abbay looked at me and then at Naren from top to bottom. Realized how much we have had his speech. Took my hand off and acted same way Naren did. I was laughing happily inside.

Chapter 9 – Knowing My Mom

The school lessons and homework became more serious. I had reached a level to skip weekend playtime almost every week. No more work outs or silly exercise with Abbay. Home works piled and I was memorising book from cover to cover. To my satisfaction grabbed first rank, unfortunately it affected my health.

After going to doctor, he confirmed that I am suffering from Typhoid fever. For the next two weeks, I got instructions to stay inside home and take as much rest as possible. Mom worried a lot and she took two weeks leave from her bank job. Dad too took couple of days off from his college lecturer work.

Both were extremely cautious of what I eat and made sure my health gets better. I got attention from everyone. The way mom stayed with me always was highly comforting and joyful. No need to go to school, no home works, no punishments, no pressure of marks. Probably everything I used to dream about at that age.

Mom will keep Aryan or Abbay a little away from me. Abbay didn't know what to do or what to tell for me. He will come, visit me, and give his class work note to mom for copying. First, he bought Vasundara's note book as her hand writing will be very good. But I was reluctant that mom should use only Abbay's note. Mom found it very difficult to understand inscriptions somehow, she managed.

Recovery was faster than I expected. Two weeks passed by and mom allowed me to play inside the house. Only indoor games like chess, carom board. We were also fine with it, because of what happened last time when we played cricket. We were playing snakes and ladder, dad begun a conversation with grandpa.

'You have skipped insulin injection, dad. Take it immediately' a rare very serious tone from dad.

'My memory is getting dimmer day by day.' Grandpa said nodding his head.

Abbay entered the conversation slowly. 'If we do exercise everyday then no need of tablets.'

Dad acknowledged him. 'Yes, Abbay. That's correct. But, Grandpa has diabetics and he is too old. He must take medicine regularly. It is inevitable as we get old.'

'Uncle, I wasn't talking about grandpa. I am telling for Akhil and Aryan, then you and aunty. This severe disease came to Akhil only after he avoided playing, doing exercise and became a typical first bench book worm. Aryan almost every month gets cold or fever, mainly because he never does any physical work.'

Dad was thinking on the point Abbay trying to make. Mom cleaning the show case shelf suddenly interrupted 'Why did you include me and uncle in the list? We are healthy.'

'Yes, for now. Both of you do rarely any physical work. When you get old and hair starts to become white, you will also end up like grandpa taking lot of pills and regularly visiting doctors. The doctor will tell you walk at least an hour daily. Instead of getting sick and then based on doctor's advice doing walking, you both can start now and be healthy in old age.'

Dad and mom looked at each other. Dad chuckles looking for an answer 'Abbay, your friend was simply infected by viral fever. Physical work has nothing to do with it.'

Mom with a very stern tone 'He is right and he got a point.' Dad knows the meaning of that firm voice, so smiled and turned around. I was very happy for a moment. Mom disliked Abbay and now she just accepted his argument. On the other hand, dad and grandpa were extremely unhappy as he defined them.

Mom went back to kitchen and came back after couple of minutes 'what did you mean by *"he avoided playing, doing exercise"*? When Akhil was doing exercise?'

Straightened by back bone, eyes went big and trying give some sort of signal to Abbay. Abbay understood that my mom was uninformed about karate practises at the ground. He gently replied 'Aunty, I was talking about warm up rounds and stretching we do before playing'

I kept my head down, so did Abbay as both knew mom would somehow figure out the truth on seeing our face.

At dining table on dinner time, mom politely asked me 'Why did you stopped playing and gave too much importance to studies?'

The timing of question surprised me as usually mom never talks when we eat. 'This year's subjects were little tough and I got heavy competition from Safina and Vasundara. It was difficult to get first rank and hence put more effort on studies and reduced play.'

'Getting first rank that much important to you?' little firm voice and volume increased.

Only confused by her question. I thought mom wanted me to be first in everything. Took a little time to give proper answer to that 'Not the most important thing. If I get first rank, except for Abbay everyone will praise me, strangers will become friends, play with me and I will attain a stardom status.'

Though I carefully phrased each word still caught by mom. '" *Except Abbay?*" assume it includes us too.'

Kept my head down, nodded and in a hussy voice 'You too will smile more and spend more time with me when I get first rank.'

Mom became very sad. Dad was trying to explain they are so proud of him irrespective of what rank I get. Mom was not talking and I worried by the expression on her face. After dinner mom came closer to me and I kept my head on her lap.

Mom combed my hair with her hands, smiled when I looked at her. 'Sorry, it was my mistake that you took first rank so serious because of me.'

'Not because of you, just to get respect from everyone at school' to ensure she feels better.

As usual with a glowing smile, 'it's ok for me whatever rank you get. I know you are intelligent and smart. You should balance time between studies and playtime. I want you to properly utilize your abilities and talent, that's all.'

It concerned me that I had hurt her because of this. Wanted to move on from this topic, so gave cute smile and nodded my head.

'Ok, after a month you can go with Abbay to practise karate. Every day you must study and play, just should properly balance it. And tell your friend he is neither good in keeping secrets nor in telling lies.' Mom chortled.

Stood up in excitement and hugged her. Mom turned around towards dad and Akhil, 'From tomorrow you both are going for walking either in the morning or evening without fail every day.'

She said that in such an authority, both knew "*No*" is not an option. Both looked at each other and nodded head with a creepy smile. Already today dad was unhappy by the fact that Abbay question him and because of him he got into this.

From the next month, I went for karate. Abbay used to fight with boys taller than him and believe they were studying college. He always practices punching and kicking above his head for this reason. He is now a holder of three belts already, whereas I am fresher.

Apart from weekend play time, I have ever day at least an hour to play. Mostly it will consist of me, Abbay, Aryan, Naren, Nirmal, Vasundara and Anjali. If it was a team sport usually Anjali will take Abbay side. I will try my level best to get into his team, sometimes succeeded.

I found it very difficult to have a private conversation with Abbay, as either Vasundara or Anjali will be always around him. I was at a discomfort at times. Inside I always had the fear that Vasundara will become closer to Abbay than me.

We all knew Abbay as very tough child. Whatever the punishment he got or beating, I had never seen him cry till date. He does get angry, very rarely. All our assumptions and perceptions about him turned out wrong one evening.

We are playing some indoor games. Don't remember exactly what it was. Then decided to relax and we are giving company to grandpa, who was watching a very old movie of 50s in TV. The movie was very melodramatic, highly sentimental, and emotional.

A howling sound came near me. Surprised and very slowly turned towards my left shoulder. Abbay was crying and everyone in my family surrounded us. They were asking, what's the reason behind it? Abbay was wobbling his head as a sign to say no and pointed towards TV.

Everyone was tittering and trying to explain it was just a movie. Even Aryan teased him. None of this helped Abbay though. He cried louder and louder as they tried to calm him down. I was still at shock and gave him a glass of water. It's hard to believe he is crying, that too for a silly emotional scene in a movie. He almost cried for half an hour.

The next day at school, Abbay was explaining how emotional the movie was to last bench boys. I am looking at him surprised and laughing inside.

Couple of weeks went by. On one occasion teacher caught Abbay and Vasundara talking in the class. Our teacher decided to punish both severely. Abbay tried his level best to convince miss that he only asked for rubber and she hasn't spoken back or done anything wrong. Miss was not ready to accept. Abbay pleaded to punish him only and leave her.

Finally, both got penalty to stand on the bench for next two periods. A period at that was 45 minutes, I guess. Vasundara now been this long friend of Abbay, used to these punished and did make a fuss about it. She stood immediately on the bench. Out of option Abbay stood gloomy.

The next period was sports hour and we all went out, except the two on the bench. When we came back, we saw Abbay crying and Vasundara trying to console him with a water bottle in hand. The teacher looked scared and she was trying to figure out why this boy is crying. None in the school till date had seen him cry even on toughest physical punishment.

Two hours on bench is like having bread and butter for morning breakfast for him. The teacher finally came to realization he was crying because Vasundara got punishment due to his actions. Miss was smiling and she was teasing Vasundara for Abbay's behaviour.

Seriously everything happened in the past month made think that do I really know my best friend? It was a completely new side of him, being highly emotional. I always believed he was very ashamed of crying in front of others. Wrong again. He never ashamed or felt bad about it, "*if I feel like crying, I will cry. There is nothing wrong in that*" that was his reply. Strange, but true, he too feels pain just little different.

Chapter 10 – Another Possible Friend

During the summer holidays, new family shifted next to our home. Two girls of our age were there in the family. In that one girl's name is Keerthika. Within couple of days, twice I saw her outside of the home, sitting with head rested on closed door and crying. I felt peculiar the way she used to be alone and behave with attitude. She became friend of Vasundara and came with her to play.

I conveyed my displeasure of her joining with us to Abbay. 'Hey, I have a wired feeling of the new arrival Keerthi in our play team.'

Abbay confused and his face shrink 'Who is Keerthi?'

'I mean Keerthika, the girl who stays next to my house. That lean needle face' told as if I completely hate her.

'Ohh... She became Keerthi? And lean needle face?' teasing me. 'Yes, short form of Keerthika. Can't short Abbay name, right? If someone is lean, what's wrong in telling?' yelled at him.

'Ok, Ok, calm down. I was just kidding. Yes, she is showing some attitude. But I think all girls are like that only, initially. Once became friends, they are much easier. She is just a kid like us. She will come along, give her some time,' patting on my shoulder he moved forward.

'I never considered you as kid, you are like grandpa' murmured within myself.

'What? What are you saying to yourself?' he enquiringly grabbed me.

'Just was telling myself, another Vasu is getting for you' pushing him away from me.

'Well, you never know. I can smell smoke out of jealous' cunningly he replied. Both ran towards others and team separation happened. So far in any games or sports we played, winning is just to keep the competition spirit alive. We all play for the fun. It was all about winning for Keerthika. Sometimes she will go far and cheat, though she never agreed it.

Many occasion big arguments broke out between Keerthika and me/ Abbay. Vasundara carefully remained at bay, instead of taking a side and always stayed out of it. Each passing day I hated Keerthika more.

Abbay usually cut people from our gang, if he feels uncomfortable. Twice he spoke to Vasundara about Keerthi's behaviour. Vasundara requested Abbay to give her little more time. Just because of his second-best friend's request, Keerthi stayed in our gang.

One night around 7 pm, was coming back from Sphere ground with wooden bat and tennis ball. At the children's park on the corner bench, a little girl was sitting alone and weeping. From distance I could recognize that slim needle body.

The eagerness to know why she always sit alone cry; curiosity was developing all time. Today I decided to ask her, why she is such a cry-baby? Sat next to her on the same bench and trying to ask her what happened.

She unexpectedly hugged me 'I don't want to go home; aunt will beat me more and can't bear pain anymore.'

I was shaking and inexperienced on how to react or what to do in such scenario. She kept on saying the same thing repeatedly. Meanwhile I was trying to stabilize myself to handle the situation, simply expecting Abbay to come around or some adult known face to help me out of this.

Couple of minutes passed by and I slowly removed from her hold. 'If your aunt beat, tell that to your mother. She will handle,' possibly the politest talk till date I had with her.

She cleaned her tears by a handkerchief. 'My mother and father are with God. Father died before I was born and mom died when I was two months old, they told me. I stay with my father's brother family.'

She gave a big gap and for a moment the thought of being without mom and dad haunted me. Realized how hard it will be for her. But, the cruelty in me had the better of me. I thought in most absurd manner and slowly questioned her, 'Had you done anything wrong like break something costly or theft....' the worst question to ask anybody in such situation, I guess.

I still feel bad about that day for such a stupid act. I was only thinking about how she showed attitude, how she was trying to cheat and never accepts her mistakes. Before finishing the question, she looked at me in the eye 'I am not a bad girl and I am not a thief' from crumbling tone to sharp voice.

'I was washing plates in the kitchen sink. Aunt complained one of the plates had washing powder in it. I told her that will wash again. But she got furious and pushed my hand into fire.' She showed her hands.

The upper layer of the skin was black and burnt. I could see some scars on the other hand. Irrespective of whatever a child had done, I felt this was a very cruel punishment. Realized how bad she might be feeling. I stood up 'Why are you sitting here, you have to go to doctor? This is a very serious wound.'

'She will punish me more because she has to pay for doctor fee and medicine. I just have to bear and cry for few more days.'

I had to do something for this. I was impotent to bear the heat, when grab a cup of tea or coffee that is little hot. She had her hand on open fire, how can she bear that much of pain?

'Ok, come to my home. My mom will have some first aid kit. She will treat you.' I wiped her tears.

'This wound will go away soon. If you can help me, can you please ask your mom for some food and bring here? I hadn't eaten any food from morning, feeling very hungry.'

I felt pity for her. 'You can come to my home and have food as much as want. First let's go to my home.'

'If my aunt came to know about it, she will keep me outside of home. Last time when she did that, some big scary men took me to a van and have taken something out of my stomach. I couldn't walk and took rest for a month. She will torture more when I get sick. No, Akhil. Please bring food here.'

My imagination failed to see of what she has gone through. Somebody took something from her stomach? She stayed alone outside home for how long? How long she was there without food? Everything seems to be a mystery.

'Trust me, it will be our little secret. No one will know and no one in my family will tell your aunt. Please trust me and come to my home.' Snatched her hand and dragged.

Half-heartedly she came with me. 'Sit on the sofa, I will bring my mom.' Went to kitchen and explained everything to mom. She ran towards Keerthika and took a deep look at her hand. 'Mom, someone taken something from her stomach too,' whispered.

Mom treated her left hand while she was eating with the right hand. First mom nursed her left hand. She noticed the wound on her eating hand. Mom grabbed the plate from Keerthika and started to feed her. Tears almost came from mom's eyes and Keerthika was crying and smiling.

The scene was touching, I was thinking about how to give punishment to her aunt. Keerthi left our home after some time and thanked me lot. I was enquiring mom and dad whether we can complain to police or do something.

Both in harsh tone asked me to mind my own business and help Keerthi when she needs. Leave adults business to adults.

My mom and dad always wanted to stay out of trouble. No wonder they are going to keep away from this. Even after a week, I was furious and frustrated that I was incapable of doing anything to keep her away from hurt. Discussed with Abbay a couple of times about it. He checked with his father on how to help Keerthika escape torture. The only solution was to get sponsor for her and move her to orphanage located next to sphere ground.

I was disappointed that no one is willing to help the poor little girl. I was thinking and believing constitutional law will help us from these. But, the general perception of people is going to law for justice is time consuming, costly, and troublesome business. They were right partially and can't blame them much either.

On very next day, again argument and fight between Keerthi and Abbay. I was utterly disappointed by her actions. On the way to our home, we were discussing about the hide and seek game we lost and put complete blame on Keerthi.

'Abbay, she might be having very hard time at her home. I don't think she is going to change or adjust and play. Yes, I pity her. Including her in our play is a mistake. She is spoiling everything.'

Naren and Nirmal both accepted my suggestion and Vasundara was partially with us. No option for Aryan, he must take my side. Abbay was still thinking and a dull look on his face.

'Hey, she wants to win. That's all. She is not evil or something very bad. Is there any place or game where she can win? If she plays with her cousin sister, she must lose. Only here she thinks us as friends and here she wants to win. Imagine yourself in her place, no parents, beaten up every day and no one is there to tell what is right or wrong, what you guys will be today?'

'We all know you are good talker and always convince us by speaking something that inscrutable. Ok, now we are trying to say what is right and wrong, is she listening? I think our approach hopelessly failed.' Yelled at a very high volume, Keerthi might have heard that from her home.

'We tried to tell and failed, because each day she was under extreme stress. In a normal environment, she might be able to accept us. Ok, we are all blaming her "*always want to win!*" ask yourself what we are trying to do? The same. If win or lose is the same for you, then what is your problem in losing to her?'

Though the question was cent percent valid, I am going to disagree to his philosophy this time and getting firm on my argument. 'You are one who talk about righteousness, honest and loyalty. Now, you want us to lose to her knowing she is cheating us?'

'Cheat is a big word, Akhil. You are getting over cooked by this. She will listen to us once she trusts us. I still think she is different from Safina; she knows how to mingle and move with others. The environment she is in keeps her like this. If we honesty consider her as friend, we should back her now.'

'Personally, in my opinion both Safina and Keerthi are the same. Ok, what you want us to do? Accept she is not cheating and always let her win?' in more firm voice.

Abbay cleared his vocal 'Yes, we will do this for one week. If she ignores to listen to us even, then...' he paused and everyone was looking at him. 'You all can beat me!'

'What's in it for us beating you? Only our hands will hurt. If she is arrogant and ignorant after a week, you hold the responsibility of sending her out and making sure that she never interrupts us while playing' Naren logically gave a common solution.

We all accepted it and no point of wasting more time and argue. We begin a little race to home and were having fun again. Before leaving Vasundara hugged Abbay and told 'You are really amazing. Lucky to have you as friend, you are the only person to think from her position. I am sure your approach will work. You are something very special, Bye!'

Abbay gave the same unexplainable expression smiling. I grabbed him around neck 'Stop flying too high bro, ok?'

'Stomach burning?' Abbay chuckled. 'Definitely not! Feeling pity for you too' we all laughed and ran home.

In the next couple of days as expected, there is change in Keerthi's behaviour. She was listening to Vasundara and me. Instead of expected behaviour of getting close with Abbay, she got closer to me. They were still fighting. They fought for very silly things and it was fun for us.

Keerthi spent most of the time with us and rarely went to her home. She came with us to Sphere ground, sat at the corner with books and wait for us.

She requested our karate head to sit around the arena when we practise. She tries her level best to ignore practise sounds and actions.

Abbay was getting invincible at the tournaments. Next year he represented our school at district level and bought all the trophies in athletics. Our sports master was having big plans for him to take him for national levels and always insisted one day he will become Olympic gold medallist for sure.

For him the medals and praise were insignificant. He, as always wanted more challenge. These champions are no more challenging him. He still wanted to run with big boys, play and compete with them.

Keerthi became very close to my mom and Abbay's mom. Abbay's mom was a brilliant cook and everyone nearby gets tips from her. Keerthi loved to spend time with them and help in whatever manner possible. This made her aunt more vigilant. She tried to keep her within home and torture. She threatened neighbours that she will move to court for legal action if anyone tried to give false allegations with respect to Keerthi.

Abbay father gave an idea for Keerthi to check with the orphanage and move there. To convince her aunt, he suggested saying that someone is paying as sponsor for Keerthi's food and clothes at the orphanage and her aunt won't need to send a paisa. Also, this will avoid any legal troubles in future.

The idea of not spending any money for Keerthi really made her aunt interested in this proposal. Her aunt did a good though out process and finally decided to agree for it. They decided to leave the town and go back to Keerthi's aunt home. Only Keerthi's uncle was very sad and disliked the idea of leaving her like an orphan. He had no choice and must agree the deal.

Keerthi went to orphanage and she was feeling like home. She as usual, spent more time with us and at our home. She became part of our family. One thing remained the same, quarrel between Abbay and her. Though it was friendly and more of ways of showing care for each other, it still looked for funny from the outside.

Couple of years based and now the time came to change the school. It became a tradition there to move for either one of the best schools in town for sixth standard. My parents are planning to put me in OIN school because it's has produced more state rank holders over the years.

Keerthi was little worried as any one of the two schools' costs more. Girls studying along with her in the orphanage got sponsors for her studies. She was the only one left out. She discussed with us and I was thinking about checking with my parents for her sponsorship.

I had bigger problem than hers. OIN school is too costly for Abbay. His parents were planning to KDPS School which is the second best. He may also get discounts/scholarships through sports activities. Vasundara's father got transfer and she is moving away. Naren and Nirmal will join Abbay, leaving me alone.

After playing cricket, we are getting ready to leave home at Sphere ground. I wanted to talk with Abbay alone and carefully sent others away.

'Abbay, is there any possibility you can join in OIN?'

'No, it is too costly. Dad can't afford it, Anjali also requesting to change wherever I go.'

'I want to study in the same school as you guys.'

'Don't worry. You will get new friends at new school. Also, not like we are never going to meet again. Every day and weekend play time are there.'

'I want to go to school and study with you guys.' Stressed a little to make sure he understands me. 'Well, you can check with Naren and Nirmal. I believe their parents can afford the term fee.'

'No, I want to go school with you' more like shouted at him. We were smiling and looking at each other for minute. 'If it means that much to you, then you can tell your mom.'

'That's right. I must convince my parents. Give me an idea that I can put in front to make them accept.'

'Just go to your mom and tell that I want to study with Abbay.' He casually said like as it is the simplest task in the world. 'It will only back fire. Mom hates you. And thanks to you, dad and grandpa directly asked me to keep distance from you. Nobody is going to give importance to Aryan.'

'First of all, you don't need to convince everyone in the family. You just have to convince your mom, the decision she takes is going to the final verdict.'

I was unprepared to listen to his entire speech. Stopped him right there. 'Yes, that's correct. How can I convince mom? I assure you, she may not be showing it, but she too wants to discontinue your friendship.'

'I am sure your mom will agree.' that was a slap on the face for me. My blood pressure went mountain high. 'Stop teasing me on this. Just get on to the point'

'Ok, your mom might sound strict and dominant. But all she does is take care of everyone in the family, trying to direct you guys in the right direction. Your dad trusts her with his life and acknowledges every decision she makes, be it money related or health or anything. It may look like your dad has been undermined, he just believes your mom is better at making...'

'Ok, stop your philosophy and strategic analysis on my family. Get on to our business at hand.' Lost patience completely and want a solution right now. 'First you need to improve on being patience. More than anything else what matters to your mom is your happiness. Just tell her that you will be happy if you go along with me. Stop thinking too much, keep it simple.'

I was thinking about some big plans. I was thinking of creating melodrama scene, sentiments, plea, blackmail, fasting, etc., to convince mom. This fool is asking me to keep it simple, unbelievable. 'Are you telling this with your conscious? Are you sure this is going to work?'

'Trust me. I have utter faith in it.'

'What if...'

'Do you trust me?' Nodded my head and we raced home.

Plenty of thoughts were going on my mind about how to tackle mom's questions. In a very confused state of mind, decided to go with my stupid friend's suggestion. Mom was reading a book and dad was sleeping. While I entered the room, mom whispered to go out.

I have now one person less to deal, gained little confidence.

'Akhil, now tell me.' Maybe she is very dominant or it looked like that to me, the tone was very clean and sharp the way she asked me.

'Mom, I know you and dad want me to study in the best school available. As grandpa say in which school I study has less significance, it will be always upon me learn and keep my discipline. If you allow me to go school with Abbay, will gain more knowledge and will also be happy. I had learnt many good things from him, including having the guts to stand and speak the truth. I really want to spend more time with him, learn more good habits, cherish life, and improve skills. Please consider before taking the decision.'

I was unsure whether I conveyed the message correctly. Thinking about what I had done and wondering what would be her reaction. She softly told 'If it really matters to you studying where Abbay does, then ok. I will talk to dad and finalize.'

It was unbelievable. Full of surprise and thrill, hugged mom very tightly. Wow! Even on my best dreams never imaged it would be such an easy task. Jumped as high as I felt like grown taller than mom.

The joy was overwhelming. Can't deny the bitter truth, I seriously misunderstood mom even now. All the way along I thought my judgement on at least my family members would be right. It's never easy when someone proves you are thinking wrongly. Even it was your admirable best friend, it does haunt you. That day I had decided never to be judgemental about anybody or least try to have an open mind.

Chapter 11 – The Challenge

Another a new year, new school, new class, and new teachers. The same old last bench, thanks to our height. We four Naren, Nirmal and Abbay sat together again. Girls' strength was less to boys and Keerthi sat on first bench of girl's row.

First day looked entirely different. The total strength of our class was 78, 48 boys and 30 girls. The benches were long. Maximum of four grownup members can sit in a bench normally. There are only 13 benches. Girl's row will have 6 benches and desks fixed for them. They can sit freely. Our fate was worst. In every bench seven members, except for last bench boys.

Our class teacher seemed to be funny. The first problem came when we are taking notes from teacher. The space was very less to keep our note and write. We tried our best to figure out how to write properly. It looked ridiculous and it amazed us to see how seven boys on a single bench managing. Being thinner has definite advantage here.

Then we opened our book for reading comprehension, again trouble hit us. Somehow, we managed the first day. Unlike my expectations for a first day at school, a new experience all together.

On daily evening report to mom, only spoke about what was good and left this space/bench problem. Aryan meanwhile found it little odd to go alone and requested someone to come with him to drop and pick from school.

Abbay knew few seniors and he was very keen to get their suggestion on how to solve writing and reading space problem. We finally figured out few tricks after couple of days. While writing if all six keep the notebook in cross slant position at 90 degrees, we can manage. For reading only four of us will take the book out and pass to others when their turn comes.

Writing was little difficult initially, slowly everyone became accustomed. Shared reading helped us taking fewer notebooks to school. We used to take a lot of notebooks in bag. We felt that lessons and home work are little too heavy.

A couple of days before our mid-term test. A teacher got irritated, by boys talking while taking the lesson. We were hoping for new kind of punishment. He came fiercely and slapped them very hard. He attacked them like a raging bull. Couple of boys cried a lot and others were silent.

We looked at each other, horrified. Abbay, the strongest of us was thinking 50 rounds in our 1KM long ground will be impossible. In fact, he was practising for 10 rounds before start of the school itself. He was unaware of what's coming. Throughout the day, we looked petrified and were very silent than any other normal day.

Teachers beating students was common thing at that time. If students complain about teachers to parents, they will say *"You might have done something wrong, that's why he beat you."* The teachers will justify their action with proverb *"Soare the rod and spoil the child!"*

We knew very well, eventually our day will come. As expected, last bench boys blamed for noise when teacher was absent and we got slaps and hit by wooden scale on fleshy parts of hands and legs. Except Abbay, everyone cried. He simply had a grim face to show his disappointment.

Some teachers were against beating us, some of them used old methods to kneel and run. They ask to run for 2 rounds. If Naren and Abbay felt lazy or boring, then will intentionally talk and get punishment to kneel or run for 2 rounds. They go out to enjoy, have fun while running and will come very brisk with lots of energy. Others including me completely against this idea and stayed out of trouble.

Abbay caught eyes of sports master here too. Our sports master had some different plans for him after looking at his karate skills. I guess Abbay was holding black belt, which means he is an expert. The way Abbay moved and his stamina is simply unmatchable any of his age or twice of his age.

Sports master decided to train him for boxing matches, district level for Abbay's weight. Abbay also liked the idea of getting sponsorship, which can be huge amount if he wins. Also, as encouragement school will nullify his fee. This means he can help his family and spend more for Anjali.

He went to the first tournament and in his weight category, he won gold medal. The highlight was most of them knocked out in the first round itself. Only the final match went to 4 rounds as they say. We were thinking his image will go better now. We were wrong.

Our class teachers showed their displeasure in Abbay skipping many classes for his participation in sports. They always found a way to insult or beat him, even when he was right. Our opinion or point of view become irrelevant and we will never get a chance to defend ourselves. If a teacher thinks we did something wrong, its final decision.

One-day teacher beat Abbay so severely that the wooden scale itself broke. Everyone was shocked and expected Abbay to at least plea. Mostly when we plea and ask for forgiveness, the beating will be less. He was stubborn not to do that.

If he feels he there is nothing he had done wrong, he will try to defend his action and if he has done something wrong like talking with others on class hours, he will simply accept his mistake and take punishment. Either case, it will prompt teacher to get angrier and beat him more.

All these physical punishments were applicable to boys alone. Girls are free from any physical punishment. Teachers gave them additional home works or ask to write staff's notes of lesson or manage attendance sheet. They were not punishments. Honestly, they encourage girls with additional responsibilities.

In most cases I escaped from punishments or scolding. Since, I am the rank holder, everyone will go easy on me and I used to have special privileges. When they lashed out all last bench boys or when whole class involved in something, I too should suffer the punishments.

Whenever I kneel or getting beaten, hate burns within me to see girls laughing and enjoying. Always wondered why this partiality? Now the respect for my earlier teachers became sky high as they were less partial between girls and boys.

This was the primary reason I kept a little distance from all girls in the class. Till 5th standard speaking with a girl or playing with them was normal. Now, suddenly there is an enormous difference. Some of the girls avoided boys, behaved differently. They will try to talk nicely with me, only with Keerthi I will speak freely.

The teachers too unusually praise girls for everything. Yes, they got good marks and there was no girl in our class who will get below 60 marks. Teachers insult boys mentioning about ranks.

On one such occasion, Abbay smartly changed the conversation by mentioning that the 1st rank holder is still a boy. Miss tried to argue, but the records were in favour of us. Finally, Miss gave a challenge that a girl from this class will get 1st rank. Abbay cunningly replied, unless teachers purposefully reduce my marks, I am impossible to beat.

It always felt good for me, when Abbay stood beside me or praised me for whatever reason. When he trusts me like this and voting for me, my smiles are big and my blood was pumping high. At last, challenge accepted, with a straight fight in studies between me, Keerthi and couple of other girls.

The marks are standard, unlike sky high marks in the previous years. The first rank person used to get overall percentage around 90-92. Only 95 plus is achievable in maths. Other subjects if you get 80 percent and above, it is very good mark.

When exams get closer, I got a little worried and starting to fear a little on looking the way these girls are studying all the time. Abbay was fully confident and sure I am going to raise boy's dignity in the class forever. When he finds out I am little low on confidence, he will give either tell boring philosophies or exactly required tonic to fuel me.

I was thinking he is using me very well and knows exactly how to manipulate me. He can make me do whatever he wants.

Exam results came and I was lagging in language subjects and social science. Boys in the entire class were sad and lost confidence. Abbay was still cherishing and enjoying, because he got excellent marks. It seemed to be like he had forgotten the challenge.

Then the next paper came, science and I got the first mark. Now I am equal in marks with one more girl for 1st in overall total. Last hour of the day is maths and tension increased for everyone in the class. I am more worried than anyone else.

'Akhil, relax. Be cool and calm.' Abbay put his arms around my shoulder and gave a little pat.

'Easy for you to say.' Grave look and serious tone.

'I knew it you are going to get first rank and every boy in the class will give a big cheer. I am fully confident about it.'

There was no negativity in his thought or speech. He was clear and sharp on his thought. I was less confident. 'What if, I get less mark than her?'

'You won't. I bet my life on it.'

Hearing that chuckled and it felt nice. The next second when I turned away, Keerthi and my closest competitor girl (*forgot her name*) were having fun. They were giving impression as if they had already won this challenge.

'What if I lose? The humiliation in front of all girls. Might have disappointed all boys' hope. Will bring shame to each one of us, especially you.'

'No, no. You are wrong. I am very proud of you. You had already proved that you are the best in studies.'

A shock followed with confusion. Seriously, when does this boy ever going to be clear on what he is trying to say, especially when I am in extreme pressure situation. 'When I get second rank, it means I am second best in studies and winning does matters.'

'You are the best in studies. Language teachers purposefully reduced marks on your essay to make you lose in the challenge. This means they are afraid that you are going to be on top, you won there already. Even after that, yet you stand here in with a chance to win the challenge. According to me you had already won this battle.'

'Battle? You are my best friend. Anyway, you will support me only. But, think about other boys, what they feel?'

'They will be as proud of your achievement as I am. None of the boys are in shot for top 10 ranks. Only you and they all know you fought till the end against all the odds. It's more than enough for them to respect you, if respect is all you are after.'

'Why are you again and again sound like a war? This is just an exam.' Increased my tone and yelled in displeasure.

'Exactly, that's what I am trying to say. This is just one exam and not a war. So, take it easy, just think this like any other match we play at ground. Win or lose makes no difference, what we leant, the new skills we developed those alone matters.'

'You are good talker. I will give you that,' looked around at all the boys and I can feel all eyes are on me.

After a heavy deep breath 'If I get 1st, they too get inspired and next time more boys will be in top 10'.

'That's my Akhil. Now you are talking. You inspired them already. All these girls studied all day, may be some nights without sleep. Yet they are struggling to keep up with you, who everyday played, enjoyed, learning karate and spend 1/10 time with books.'

At last laughed out loud. 'You know somehow you make me feel better, irrespective of those unpractical talks.' Both smiled at each other and eagerly awaited maths Sir's arrival.

After a couple of minutes, he turned around 'Why am I excluded from those inspired persons list?' questioned curiously.

'I know you never want to be a rank holder. Marks, percentage never mattered to you. Only learning. You never memorise or study every day. Probably an hour on the exam day and get 80 to 85 percentages with ease.'

'Well, buddy. You know me, I will give you that' both laughed and suddenly all boys stood up and greeted "*Good Evening!*" to the maths teacher.

The moment he came in, he realized something is different. He looked for a minute, steadying himself from the overwhelming reception he got just now.

Abbay was the person with first role number always and teacher called his name. Though on all other subjects he fell short of 90, maths is a piece of cake for him. He got 100 again, the third time this year. He got a big round of applause and the way boys clapped made our teacher shuddered, sensing some danger.

He juggled across the benches and happily gave the paper to me. It's a usual habit of us to exchange papers and see how the other guy has answered the questions. I am in no mood to look over. Anyway, he got cent percent, all answers were perfect, what do I have to look deep into it?

The tension surrounding the class was at its peak. Boys and girls keenly waiting for my marks. Some of the boys were biting nails, some of them praying to God. Some boys hide their head inside the desk. On looking at these pictures, it alarmed me. Of course, prayed to God and hoped for a 100.

Then the boy next to me, laughing and chatting with Naren like there is nothing going on. It was just another answer paper for him, cool as a cucumber. Teacher called my name and from the moment I got up and went forward, each girl and boy were looking at me. I tried my level best to walk normally towards the teacher.

The teacher patted on my shoulder and said "Good job, Akhil. You got 98 marks."

I stood stunned and my face shrunk. For a moment, it was like the time had frozen and nothing is moving around me. Suddenly jolted hearing a thunder of applause and cheer from all the boys. To my greatest surprise, I missed 100 marks and yet every boy in my class is cherishing? I felt they are far from realizing the reality, if the other girl gets a 100, we will lose the challenge.

I walked very slowly with little smile on my face. Boys from corner side on the bench came towards me to congratulate. My teacher stood and made a conscious effort to keep them at bay. He sensed something huge is to unfold.

When I sat on the place, I can still see Keerthi and her friend laughing at me. It was like in movies, when I saw them, my nerves are breaking out and water boiling with big bubbles inside my body.

'Hey, super buddy! You had done it again. Congrats!!' Abbay laughed and hugged me.

I begin to think he is also blind to see the fact. Giggled and nervously replied 'Thank you. What if she gets a 100?'

'Come on, Akhil. Enjoy the moment, you already done it.' As usual with a tap on me, he grabbed my paper and looking what was the mistake.

The moment came when teacher called my challenger's name, everyone was on their edge of the seat and cautiously looking at the paper in maths Sir's hand, except for one. The genius next to me was looking at my wrong answer to a 2-mark question and checking with his paper. I decided to look at what Abbay doing as I can't watch it anymore.

She got the paper and her face turned blue. The teacher said "Good job. You got 96 marks." All boys shouted and a big thundering applause almost shacking our old classroom building. They chanted in chorus my name and the teacher felt hapless. Students and teachers from other classes around us came out to look what's happening.

I gave a sign of big relief, closed my eyes, and took a deep breath. The volume increased after a minute as teacher tried to control the noise. All boys came and congratulated me. I tried to act as normal as possible with a polite smile. I strongly believed that I should behave like Abbay on high and low. Kept my cool and acknowledged them.

It took 10 minutes for things to settle down. Suddenly remembered what Abbay did after winning overall championship match, greeting the runner up. I turned around and looked at her. She smiled and with action wished me for my success. In the same sign language said thank you and greeted her for performance in exam. Next to them Keerthi was all smiles and greeting me continuously.

That's the moment realized the obvious truth, that there are no boys and girls partially when it comes to friendship. She was as happy as Abbay and from her reaction, she believed in me just like him. That can be the only reason she was smiling before and now.

A day started with anxiousness and tension, ended as one of my most memorable day in life. Happy/joy/excitement, no actual words to describe that feel when everyone in the class adores and admires you.

I sometimes worried that am a lousy thinker and neglect to enjoy the moment. Went home and celebrated with my family. Then came the most absurd thought. Abbay barely studied an hour and got 80+ marks. I used to study/write for minimum of an hour and maximum of 4 hours a day only to get 10 marks more than him. What if he does the same? He might even get better marks than me.

Possibly the one only person to think like that and my eagerness made me ask this question to Abbay the next day at school.

'You considered me that I won already as I took less time and got almost marks close to them. I feel the same logic applies for us.' in a mild tone whispered around his ears when social teacher was talking about battle plans.

'Was there a competition between us? I am pretty sure you said something else than actually what you thought.' Abbay tried to whisper, I think the first bench boys heard it clearly.

'Ushhh... reduce it. My point is you never study and yet you get good marks. If you study hard, you might get first rank every time. You can try.' I still had my volume under control to ensure I am away from any trouble.

'I have no interest in getting rank one. I listen to teacher if they are telling or explaining things that are interesting. If boring or repeating same point again, I will move on to some other activity. I won't memorise, always write with my own words. If I am unable understand a concept in lessons, if will simply skip. I enjoy learning and knowing new things. Marks are only to ensure that I will stay away from torture or pressure from others. Just to stay out of trouble for others and mainly mom wants me to get above 70.'

'You could have answered in a single sentence, I might have understood.' Showing him a grim face, the essay irritated me.

'If I give a one liner, that's unlike me.' We both looked at each other and smiled.

Throughout my childhood, I always wondered, what exactly does Abbay wants from his life. He has no problem in losing, especially if you are his loved one, he will never hesitate in losing to you every time. Marks are not important to him, never worried about what others think or say about him, unless you are close to him.

What exactly is his goal? Each time when I come across a new experience, I will learn what mattered to him, so never really had to ask him that. Went on with the flow as he does and tried to keep it simple.

Before annual exams, Anjali got sick. She was suffering from Jaundice. Abbay missed couple of karate sessions and weekends play.

I was wondering what he has is doing at home for his sister's illness. Aryan too will get sick severely, but there was no hassle about it. After Sunday evening play time, went near his home to see what exactly he is doing all the time. He was slowly walking on the veranda holding Anjali in his hand. She kept her head on his broad shoulder and was sleeping.

It was nice to see such affection and it felt emotional to me. Felt disturbing either of them is wrong and carried on. Went home, had dinner and after couple of hours wanted to see him and have a conversation. Requested permission from mom to go and took Aryan with me.

Abbay was still walking slowly holding Anjali. He was patting very slowly on her head in a rhythmic manner and was whispering something to her. We both stayed hidden behind the big tree and were watching it for almost past 10 minutes without taking our eye off. Aryan hugged me tightly and we went back to home without disturbing brother and sister most affectionate emotional moment.

We used to call them *"Pasamalars' – an old Tamil movie about brother and sister affection.* The movie was melodrama, but this is real and if you really have any emotion left in you, for sure you will feel at some point and want to be like that with your brother/sister.

Chapter 12 – Invincible Boy

Anjali was back to normal in couple of weeks. There was a boxing match scheduled at school. We were so excited to watch Abbay fight in the ring. So far, we heard only the tales, the way he moves and knocks out his competitor in less than a minute. First time we are going to watch it live.

Abbay had lack of practise and sports master was furious for missing training sessions. He kept his head down and practised only on before evening. This was nothing like karate sessions or tackling. He was brutally punching sand bag and we can feel the impact though we were watching from good 100 meters away.

Couple of last bench boys were unfriendly to him. They had problem with him for being little conservative, avoids vulgar words, restricts them from disrespecting or teasing teachers. They were little afraid of his muscle strength. Abbay smartly avoided any brawl at school or away, the daring looks frightened most.

Watching the blows of Abbay, they went to restroom. Such fierce was each punch. Sports master was happy after seeing him in appropriate shape and he begun to teach on techniques. The sports master was very keen on making him move faster. Then he was practising punching above his head. It only made sense because most guys under his weight category will be taller than him.

The next day he got a huge reception coming into the ring. The seniors were chanting *"King in the Ring!!"* when he went for a handshake. This is inter-school competition and his opponent was from OIN school. He was taller than Abbay at least by a foot and he was studying 10th standard.

Me and Naren were little nervous after looking at the opponent. Nirmal having seen Abbay fight in the ring before and was very sure that this tall guy will go down in a minute. The two other boys looked shuddered remembering the scene from yesterday's practise. We came early and got place reserved on fourth row from ground.

The bell rang and huge cheer, thunder of applause and everyone stood up. I was trying to see, what was happening. Abbay was moving and punching. I can see only glimpse of the match. Barely 30 seconds might have passed, all shouted *"King in the Ring!"* and announcement came declaring Abbay as the winner.

I was extremely disappointed and frustrated on my inability to see how he fought. I slowly tried to push the guy in front of me. He turned around swiftly and fumingly looking at me. At an extreme fear of a punch, 'Sorry, brother! Just wanted to see my friend fight, didn't meant to push you.'

He was almost going to attack me and I was preparing myself to defend. Nirmal interrupted 'Brother, this is Abbay's best friend, Akhil. Abbay is very fond of him.'

Suddenly feared loomed his face and trying to hide it, he smiled at me 'It's ok, no problem' he turned away.

'He was scared' Nirmal whispered in my ears. One of the two shuddered boys slowly moved towards me 'No will dare to touch you. Yesterday at boxing practise I heard master one day challenged Abbay to take on ten guys more than 6 feet tall and he beat them like a pup. One of them surrendered to his knees scared of Abbay's punch.'

Abbay was lethal. I knew his strength and had seen it before. Inside boxing ring, I really wanted to see him move. Decided to sit on first row for the next match. This match ended because of opponent's broken ribs and unable to bear the pain anymore.

Next day I was there at ground couple of hours before the match. Forced Naren to company me and without a choice he half-heartedly came with me. As usual, the arena erupted and Abbay was walking into the ring. We were clapping with our full strength.

The match is about to begin, another taller opponent with a teasing smile. I hated that guy with all my heart. Bell rang and Abbay just moved towards him and gave a punch aimed at opponent's face. He tried to cover with his hands. Abbay gave a fierce punch on the covered gloves anyway. Irrespective of the guard the big guy felt the pain.

The next punch was on his four pack guts. Unable to bear the pain he screamed in agony and dropped his guard. Abbay moved towards his right and a big right hander on the face. Abbay gave a couple of seconds' gap and realized opponent stood, traded back-to-back punches on face, ribs, and guts.

After the mighty attack, Abbay moved away from him. The opponent fell down bleeding from mouth, few teeth gone, the mouth guard was unhelpful. The cheer was continuously rising and the opponent stayed at floor. Abbay was victorious again.

'They said for inter-district matches, you had to pay a minimum of 30 rupees to watch the tournament. I am going to go to next district tournament. It's absolutely worth to watch his guy fight.' Naren was laughing, yelling, and jumping looking at the scene.

I was looking at the big guy who had given that teasing smile looking at the height of Abbay. Chuckled and cherishing my buddy's victory. He was neither jumping nor rejoicing. He went towards the fallen guy and checked whether he was ok.

Furious by the loss, he tried to push Abbay. Abbay helped him get up and move towards the corner. The seniors were cursing, speaking inappropriate words, when the other school guy pushed Abbay. They failed to notice Abbay is helping his opponent, though his opponent pushed him.

Every time I see this guy do something like that, my respect for him increases. The tournament went on and Abbay won it with ease. Only in final it took him two rounds and the opponent retried due to broken elbow.

Apart from trophies, one private sponsor gave Abbay huge money. He was very happy and he is now actually earning to help his family. The most awaited summer holidays arrived.

Anjali was pressuring her parents to change school. She wants to go with her brother. Due to heavy expenses, her parents could convince her so far. With sponsor amount won by Abbay in boxing, they might be able to afford it. His dad agreed to his daughter's demand and school changed. She is going to come with us from next year.

Keerthi's sponsor presented a new bag for her and she was very happy. She showed to each of us and Abbay teased her. I think he adored duelling with her, something was seriously wrong between them.

I became a full-time wicket keeper in cricket matches, along with Abbay. We both were decent, close to be good. We slowly became the best wicket keepers in either of the team. Now, we are part of team every match. Because of full time team members, we will get to bat every match in the lower order. Our batting was improving steadily to the mark.

Next day we were at sphere ground and Keerthi was little dull. I took a break when others were batting. 'Hey, why are you dull? What happened?' going to be out of breath, still managed to question her curiously.

'Nothing, just another day.' She turned her face towards the ground. I knew she is lying and will tell me what happened for sure if I stay with her alone a little while. Asked her to pass the water bottle and pretended to be watching the match, drinking water slowly.

'I really want to know, who is paying for my studies.' Depressed Keerthi in frustrated mood.

'Ask at the home. Sure, they will know.'

'The sponsors feel it is best for everyone to keep it secret for two reasons. If they tell other kids, they will also ask and would want sponsor to adapt them and my sponsor promised to disclose once I finish my studies.'

The logic sounded reasonable for me. 'If they are circumspect, why are you forcing? Finish our studies, earn by yourself and then help them.'

She looked at me angrily. 'For other girls at home, each year new sponsor will come. For me they are the only sponsors for two years. They helped me when I needed the most. I would be dead by now, if they had decided to leave me.'

I felt she is creating unnecessary drama. This behaviour is the reason behind her frequent quarrel with Abbay. I was trying to make her realize that they are doing this without any expectation.

'See, they don't want you to pay back or worship them. They are helping you, because they are big hearted and good people.'

'I know. I am unable conclude myself. It's just crazy of me to thinking about returning the favours. Even I feel like I owe your parents and Abbay's, for their kindness, food and all the help.' She is even more frustrated now.

'If you are thinking about returning favours, then can stop talking to us and stay at our orphanage home itself.' Her answer irritated me and was furious.

She grabbed my hands 'No, no. Sorry! I didn't mean like that and I always want both you to remain as my friends forever. I just want to know who saved me, that's it.'

I tried to keep cool. 'You will know when your studies are completed. Stop bothering about it now. If you really want to do something back to everyone, study hard and achieve your goal.'

'You are right. I will study and become a heart surgeon one day.' She always wanted to become a doctor, especially a heart surgeon as her dad died of some problem in heart before she was born.

'I know you would want to tear people apart once grown up' chuckled and moved towards play area.

After couple of weeks, Abbay got opportunity to bowl for the first time. He ripped the top order. He was team's wicket keeper batsman already and now key bowler in the team. I got promotion in the batting order and moved to play at one down.

I was consistent scoring runs at all the games. I used to score at a steady rate and strike rate was average. I had never got out in single digit score. Abbay was less consistent, he will rarely play more than 10 balls per innings. On his day, he might take any bowler apart and score at a strike rate of more than 200. Whenever he gets out to bat there will ball flying in the sky for sure.

We both now got new cycles to go school, from this year. Anjali came with us too. She was sitting in the front bar safely between two pillars – *Abbay's hands*. He was all smiles and we rode steadily to school. I was trying my level best to keep attention away from Anjali. Around the crossroad near signal, I went behind Abbay.

His cycle had a carrier at back, made of steel. He was riding his father's cycle. He is close to 5 feet 5 inches now and barely can ride a small vehicle. Mine was much fancier, race cycle as Aryan would call. My cycle had a very small carrier at back and possible can fit Aryan. His cycle was big and back carrier was enough for Anjali to have a good ride. I was wondering a bit about this on our way to school.

I remained silent about it as I knew Anjali forced him. He is always uncomfortable in riding if someone sits on the front bar. He was wrestling with hand bar to keep the balance and barely able to push hard, especially on the uphill from the main road. He was always relaxed riding doubles in the cycle, when someone sits behind in the back carrier. He can keep up and beat us easily if it was race. Now he is struggling to balance it and mostly going zig-zag on the road.

When reached the school, many looked at us and laughed. Abbay giggled at Anjali as she left for her class. We kept our cycle in the stand and walked towards the class room.

'You have any expectations on this year's class?' slowly inquired him.

'They say, we will get beaten by metal rods for talking, looking forward to that' Abbay chuckled and scared me to hell. My expression changed and worried about rods at least for the first couple of months before exam marks can make me escape from punishments.

'Do you really think, they will beat us with metal rod?'

'That's what I heard. You know they always extravagate things. Maybe they will beat us in finger bones or use wooden sticks in fleshy parts of leg.' He said as it was nothing.

'Do you feel pain at all? I mean every year they use new weapons or new severe punishments; you are kind of always seems to enjoy taking hits.' I think had asked him question that was in my mind for a very long time.

'They will be painful for couple of days max. Once you got used to that it will be easy.' Again, the ease at which he said made me feel scratchier.

'So, you enjoy them hitting you every day? What advantage did you got out of it?'

'No one want to get beaten. There are no advantages for me in it. Having said that, sometimes I feel it sort of helped in the ring while fighting.'

I stopped walking and looked stunned. 'Helped in boxing?' more eager to listen the answer.

'Had you ever seen me take a hit and guard? Or after a hit losing my focus?'

'No, you will stand like a feather touched you smoothly.' My tone was more for jealousy and disarray, indicating how bad I felt on seeing those fights.

'It's because I can bear the pain and ability to move on full force.'

We were walking again. For a couple of steps both were thinking the other will talk.

'I figured out irrespective of how fast you move, your skills, ability and strength, it is inevitable you are going to be hit by your opponent at some point. When your opponent has all the qualities to be equal with you, the only difference between you and him is the ability to take a hit and still stand in your feet for a fight back. In tough fights, it is never about how hard you can hit. It's always about how hard a hit you can take.'

Abbay explanation made real sense to me, yet good opportunity to tease him 'The last line should definitely be written on back of auto.'

He grabbed me and tried to choke me delicately. The fact that he is winning each match in first round is because of this theory. He is invincible in the ring, but had he never hit by opponent? No, definitely not. I recalled each match. When he gets a punch on him, he will never guard. He will try to punch with twice the force back. Some occasions he hit right on the boxing glove of the opponent when they go for a punch, one of his most signature and unique move. He does think different, that's the biggest reason for his success.

'You are uncomfortable today, riding with Anjali in the front bar of the cycle. You might ask her to sit on the back seat?' it looked as he was expecting this question from me.

'I asked her to sit on the back seat. She is little scared and wants to stay within my arms as she feels safe.' Graciously describing the scenario, we reached the classroom.

'I feel she is doing a bit too much. You?' questioned him moving towards the last bench which was a fair distance away because of bigger class room.

'She is different and always in fear. A bit like my mom, I guess. She never forces or orders me. She is very polite and ask me things very cutely that I don't get the heart to say no to her. If I will never do certain things, all I should do is deny twice to make her understand. She will understand and move on.'

'I know that no one can force or dominate you. Just felt you are too protective about her.'

'Yes, I agree' nodded his head and both kept out bag inside the new big desks.

'You have a problem in riding with one some sitting in the bar. You are riding all over today on the road. On a busy day, might have had a different result. Seriously you have to work on it, buddy.' Tried to explain him the reality.

'Obviously. I was thinking about it all the way and thought of practising' he acknowledged my suggestion.

'Practise? You are looking for a scapegoat?' trying to tease him again.

'Why you call yourself a scapegoat? I will ensure your safety while practising.' Abbay chuckled.

That one seriously back fired on me, straightened my backbone, and looked frightened as if a ghost slapped me. The teacher entered the class and we all stood up.

The first one week at school was fantastic. We got around 16 benches and desks, bigger class room and our class strength reduced by five members. They all are smooth and easy so far. Then, the punishments started. Teachers are now stricter or tried to act like that and they did beat on the finger bones with wooden scale.

Abbay continued with his excellence in sports. Looking at his game, our cricket team coach wanted him for wicket keeper. Already, he is in boxing and athletics. They restricted him to take part in more than one category.

His muscles become harder and harder, to such an extent he is no more the sprinter he was before. This was excellent opportunity for Naren and grabbed with both the hands. In 100 and 200 metres, Naren could outpace him. In 400 metres category they both were very close, neck and neck. Some existing race to watch for us. But, beyond 400 still there isn't anyone to match him. The stamina of Abbay, stood tall and he was setting record times in 800, 1500 etc.

Abbay was gaining more money as each day he passes victory. But he was little unhappy. Hard to image a boy as him being invincible at such a high stage and looking sad, strange.

We later came to know that in the last tournament he broke one boy's ribs during fighting and it resulted in heavy sufferings and expenditure for that boy. This made him feel guilty and he is now making conscious effort to evade severely injure on his opponents. Knock outs reduced and he is winning more by points now.

He got a new teacher in town who teaches mixed martial arts. He is now an expert in karate to level that he beats our karate expert with ease. The new fighting skills made him even a better boxer.

He is known for his muscle strength and fast moves; he wasn't extremely flexible till now. Tides turned and now he is strong, quick, flexible, and more lethal as he now learnt how to take out opponent without breaking their bones or hurting them too much. The idea is to hit on muscle with technique, he kept those tricks undisclosed, since he has promised to master that he will never reveal to anybody.

Chapter 13 – Favourite Teacher

Keerthi maintained lot of distance from us. Our gang now became *"Only Boys."* She came seldom to the ground. She used to sit on the park most of them time when we go for playing cricket. Around the summer holidays time, one afternoon when we are coming back to home, we saw her holding stomach and looked in some severe pain.

Me and Abbay both rushed to her. She was unable to even speak, she slowly begun to scream in agony. We forced her to come to my home and explained situation to mom. I was ready to call doctor on the next street and Abbay went to his home to call his mom.

We both were waiting outside for an hour and then our moms came out smiling and talking. We looked at each other confused, curiously went near them.

'Mom, is she ok now?' More out of eagerness to know what's happening than inquiry.

'She is good now.' Mom gave a crisp and simple reply meant no more questions. I understood the context of it, but poor Abbay can't control himself.

'What happened to her? What was the problem? Is it a side effect? Because of someone took kidney from her stomach when she was little?' Abbay was pouring in questions.

My mom looked at him, the big steaming eyes indicated she is very angry due to those questions. Abbay's mom as cool as usual, 'It's a women thing and you boys are too little to know or talk about it,' she explained as simply as she can.

Abbay was about to ask further questions. I grabbed his hand tightly indicating him that we should go by now, else we might have to face my mom's furry. On the moment of grab, he luckily noticed her face and stopped right there. We both left the house back to Sphere ground without taking our evening snack, only with couple of water bottles. He is thinking about something other than the snack; my only thought process was about missing the snack.

While we jogged back to the ground, 'You still want to know what happened to her, right?' I was expecting a yes from him.

'I know you too want to figure out as much as I do.' Abbay was sure on what he said.

Little confusion loomed around my head, realizing he got something to go with it. 'You got some clue?'

'Only noticed that my mom said, *"women matter"*.' We were running towards the big tree for shadow.

'I was looking more at my mom. Yes, that is interesting.' We both sat on the bench and got ready for a drink. I was thinking about the missed crispy potato chips.

The next day there was a kind of function at home. After inquiring with various people, the only detail we got is the function is for Keerthi – "*Attending the age.*" That phrase was blur and failed to reveal the exact meaning.

Abbay let it go after couple of attempts. I persisted in knowing the details. There was no google at that time to help us. Well, we were unaware of internet and google at that time.

My enthusiasm grew every passing minute and finally it was an old woman who tried to explain me the concept of the ceremony. I left scratching my head after her talk, the actual point I took is "*now she is grown women. She is eligible to marry and bear children.*" From our social science subject civic class, I knew girl's eligible marriage age is 18. I was thinking Keerthi is very fast and mature, she became eligible by thirteen itself.

I believe in the rest of the summer holidays much of time went through researching on this. Plenty of new things were happening around, beyond to our understanding and knowledge. Abbay as usual went to his uncle's home. This might be the last time he is going there. His uncle farming suffered severe loss for the second consecutive year. From what I heard, looks like he must find another job to survive with his two kids.

Next year at school, things were more different. Boys behaved in a usual way especially when girls are around. I had no knowledge on what flirting and blushing means then, it was just odd for me. Keerthi nowadays maintaining a fair distance from us. It seemed to be like everything is in a chaos. I felt it is better to stick with Abbay and follow him as long as I can.

The punishments were one level up. Teachers used to have specially crafted and designed sticks (*made of bamboo I think*).

Our favourite teacher was Mr. Kamalnath. He is barely 5 feet tall, very lean. His nick name was "*Skeleton*" proudly kept by a group of our seniors and they were right of course. He used to wear very lose full hand shirts, mostly they will be of brown colour. A bracelet very loose in his hands (*I think that was the smallest size bracelet ever you will find for an adult in earth, yet it was lose*). His signature style moment will be to move the bracelet from wrist to elbow by trembling his right hand. He will do that every 5 minutes once at the minimum.

He was very friendly with us. So far, there has been always a gap between student and teacher relationship, it all changed. He was very friendly and all boys were very fond of him. He was against beating or scolding us, always treated with smile. No punishments from him.

One evening before the Diwali festival, many staffs were absent at school. We had three consecutive periods without any teacher or staff in the class. After the first period, we all decided to play indoor games. At that time the popular one was book cricket. The last bench boys, we split into three teams by two in each.

The game is very simple. Each team will have 10 chances and we should open some random page in the book. If the page we opened has number ending with 2, 4, 6 we will get the same number of runs and added to the total score. If page number ends up with 8 means only 4 runs and if zero means out – *one chance over*. Only even page numbers considered, index pages or any other blanks means a dead ball.

Now it appears very childish, at that time it was all fun. I think we all were crazy of cricket; any type of the game was joy full for us. We conducted a triangular tournament, me and Abbay were close to win the finals. All other students were talking shouting, some of them were fighting I guess for some girl. We were enjoying and having fun with our little game.

The noise was such loud, our school Headmaster rushed into the class. He was yelling, scolding, and cursing us. Kamalnath Sir came a couple minutes later and he tried to take this in a smooth effortless way. Teachers from nearby classes also came into the picture once HM came into our class room.

As predicted, the last two bench boys convicted for the crime of making huge noise in the class and HM wanted to beat us for sure. Kamalnath Sir unsuccessful attempts to rescue us only triggered HM to give immediate thrashing.

HM Sir shouted in loud voice, 'Kamal Sir, either you are going to punish them or shall I tell other teachers to punish them. All other teachers are having wooden sticks. They will tear their upper skin apart, due to the anger there are in on these students.'

'Sir, look at them. They all look like beast. Only our hand will suffer trying to beat them. Let us give 2 complete rounds that cover 2 KM distance in our ground and I will ensure they run the distance.'

'These guys will run easily that distance. Especially the tallest one. I don't want to pardon them, Kamal. Look at all teachers, their time is also getting wasted by this.'

'Exactly, honourable HM. Why you all waste your precious time on these silly boys. Let me take care of them.' The nose cut was too good that everyone in the class laughed at teachers with wooden sticks. This only provoked our HM further.

'Now, are you going to teach them a lesson or shall I, Kamal?' HM told him furiously.

"Nobody is listening to me nowadays" whispered within himself and marched towards us fiercely. He was smart and always very funny. He started with the least tall boy of 12 guys standing there.

That boy was smaller and leaner than him. He grabbed his hair furiously and yelling at him, 'will you do this again?' Then he bended the boy and raised his hands. The class was in stun silence. He kept his hands such a way that a big sound will come when beats on your flesh next to spine, but it won't be painful at all.

The sound erupted and echoed. The boy plead, 'Sorry, Sir. Sorry, Sir. Will never talk again in the class.'

'Hmm.... That's! that fear should be there. Remember this hit, you will never dare to speak again even to your mom.' Saying this punch line, he made his signature move with his bracelet. Till now who ever tried to remain silent and holding their smile, couldn't resist any more after that punch line and style.

The whole class erupted in laughter. HM turned out with the angriest look on his face and everyone suddenly silenced. Kamal Sir was cool as cucumber. In fact, he wanted to avoid this punishing student and tried to make other staffs leave.

He went towards the next boy. He was little taller and close to his height. The same happened again but this time no laughter from the students. The next five guys were of similar height he managed with them. Then came the real last bench height, starting with Nirmal. He was taller than Kamal Sir. Kamal Sir gave a deep thought on how to beat this guy.

He asked Nirmal to bend forward. When Nirmal did, he was at same level to the height of Kamal Sir. He was looking at him and then turned around to the HM. The HM was unable to control his smile, so he turned towards other teachers with his hands covering the mouth.

Kamal Sir moved sideways of Nirmal and asked him to bend further. He finally gave two hits on the fleshy part close back bone. Nirmal screamed 'Enough, Sir. Enough, Sir.'

Kamal Sir showed a big relief in his face and about to make his signature style. One of staff from 10th standard at the right moment said 'Hey, you think us as fool? He hasn't even started to hit you and you are acting like he is trying to kill you? Kamal, Sir. Give him sound hard four more beats.' The teacher said with amazing conviction.

The HM laughed and Kamal Sir looked at the other staff as he had asked for 100 KG gold. His strength was gone and he slowly raised his hands to the other staff 'Why? What wrong had I done to you?' he whispered.

After a deep breath, he asked Nirmal to kneel and then bend to give couple more dummy hits, only to bring an echo. He could manage with one hit for each of the other four boys with bent knee and bent forward as lower as they can.

When my turn came HM and other staffs supported me as rank holder, it pleased Kamal Sir. Then he moved to last and final guy. The whole class, the staffs and HM were all laughing. It was Abbay, he was close to six feet and approximately two feet taller than Kamal Sir.

He looked from bottom to top and kept a hand on his back neck as he is looking at the tallest thing ever to walk on this earth. I was standing next to Abbay, trying to resist. He came close to Abbay and murmured 'Did they made you with spells or gave normal birth? I am sure you ate a lot of Complan to grow this taller.'

He asked him to bend, assume he did that on purpose to make fun. He might have simply asked Abbay to kneel and bend as he did with others. Abbay bent forward and was significantly taller, Kamal Sir tried to jump and reach his shoulder. Now everyone was laughing out loud.

'You beast. Go and stand next to Akhil.' Kamal Sir said with a smile in his face.

Looking the scene, the AHM fiercely came inside the class. 'What's so funny? You all teachers does not know how to handle these silly boys.' He took the wooden stick and slapped below knee of the first small boy standing there. The boy screamed in agony and pain, AHM was brutally moving the stick towards the next guy.

Kamal Sir ran towards him, 'Sir, you are beating these little poor fellows. Start from the biggest guy in the town, he is the main reason for all the trouble.' On doing this, we disliked our teacher briefly, but he knew that wooden stick is a mere thing to beat Abbay.

The AHM ran towards him and the first blow was mighty, Abbay felt the pain and strengthened his leg. He will never scream or plea. Four or five slaps went along, other teachers were afraid and many were unable to see this. The wooden stick broke into two halves. The AHM is out of breath. He took that as serious defeat, he went and took other wooden stick and all students in the class gave a "*ohh!*"

Our headmaster came in and tried to stop. The stick now broke in two slaps, as AHM hit on his biceps. Abbay already strengthened his muscle, still standing keeping his head down. The AHM gone out of breath and was having severe cough. He needed water to stabilize himself.

Kamal Sir now has every reason to stop this massacre, 'Please, Sir. Take care of your health as I already told you, only we will suffer if we try to beat them. The two rounds around the ground were the right choice.'

HM and others acknowledged, they cursed Abbay a lot and left the class. Mr. Kamal came to Abbay 'Extremely Sorry, pa. These poor little fellows might end up in hospital after the wrath of those teachers. I know you can bear it and to save them, I pointed you. Forgive me.'

Now the respect for my teacher went one level up. Abbay looked at our teacher 'It's nothing Sir. I am perfectly fine. Have no worries, Sir. Even if it had continued, four more sticks might have broken. If the stick stays away from my sensitive parts, I am absolutely fine.'

Kamal Sir, tapped on Abbay's back, 'that's the spirit my boy. You are really a good one, far better than all those who cursed you. You will shine and go to the top one day.' He always encourages and appreciates even when we fail. His theory of motivating students is one the rarest in the modern world.

He is one of my favourite teachers. He was simple, easy to approach, highly skilled and talent. The way he treated students was one of the rarest especially when many teachers around him treated us like slaves.

Chapter 14 – Guilty

This state level boxing tournament arrived, Abbay is the favourite as usual. He travelled for state level match at Chennai. We all gave our best wishes to him.

We have been hearing the news and built-ups of how Abbay is knocking out opponents in the first round itself. He sailed to the semi-final and everyone in the school eagerly awaited the moment for championship.

When we were all waiting to hear the result of the final round, Kamal Sir informed us that Abbay refused to take part in the final and he also never arrived at the arena to receive the silver medal. This was shocking for all of us and we questioned everyone at school office to know what happened. No one gave proper response and Kamal Sir convinced us to wait till he returns to school on Monday.

He should be at home on Saturday. I worried for him and so was Keerthi. We want to avoid triggering a panic and alarm his parents. We both know nothing might have happened to him and it ought to be something else.

Usually for going to school, he will come to my home. I decided to go early to his home and meet. Half an hour before, I took my cycle and went to his home. I am happy to see Abbay having breakfast along with Anjali. I walked across the small hall to get various angles of view at him. I want to ensure he is completely normal physically. There was not even a single scratch on him as he turned around and smiled at me.

The satisfaction of seeing him normal was enough for me. As Anjali was with him, I felt it was improper to ask him anything about boxing tournament. We were already late, so both of us were riding the cycle very fast. From cycle stand to class room we raced to avoid any confrontation from our teacher.

Around lunch time, when I finally got some time alone with him, curiously wanted to know what happened.

'Abbay, what happened at the tournament?' mild as a feather.

'In semi-final match I beat the other boy so severely that he was admitted to hospital in ICU. Multiple complex fractures and he will never be able to use his hands the same way as before. I spent the whole night and next day at hospital with him. I was feeling guilty for it and still can't really get over it.' He sounded depressed.

'Their parents scolded or cursed you?' trying to figure out more detail.

'No, I would have felt better if they had done that. They were kind and too good. His father bought me food and was trying make me understand it was just a sport and his son had a rough day. I disagreed.' He was staying away from my eyes and talking, I know this is not wicked.

'He is right of course. It's the just a sport and that's how it is. There is nothing wrong in what you did. It is a risky sport and that the reason, the winner gets special attendance, popularity and value for his struggle.' I was trying to cheer him up and his sad looks and grimness were awful and unpleasant for me.

He looked at me and chuckled. 'You are worse than me when trying to tell philosophy or wisdom. You dig at this.'

I was happy he was smiling, 'Yes and you made me do this.'

'I know the reality. This is not the first time I had broken someone's bone in a fight. Had done it many times before, all along was thinking it is just a sport and injuries are normal when you put yourself on the line in any sport. Now starting to feel little different. Yes, I am getting good sponsorship out of it. I dislike it, making money from others blood. I feel it's wrong.'

I was listening to him and nodding my head to ensure that he feels better. He continued, 'Each one of them who's bones were broken, they all can never be the same again. They must rely on someone else to eat, use restroom and at house arrest for at least three or fourth months. How hard it will be for their parents? What if it has happened to me?'

I understood the way he is feeling about fighting. He certainly wants to avoid hurting anyone anymore. The question in my mind was, why this fight had so much impact him.

'What exactly happened in the ring that day?' wanted to be clear on what kind of answer I am expecting from him.

'He is a second-year engineering student, a couple of inches taller than me. When the bell rang in first round, it was like fighting against myself. He moved fast, my hits failed to make the same impact as it did on others, he came back hard after each punch. Both kept our guard down in the first round. We were only trading punches and he looked very energetic after that round. At last, I was feeling I got a real challenge at my hands. This match will tell what I am. I believe he was thinking the same. I heard he used knock everyone in first round and coach planning for next common wealth games championship for him.'

Abbay gave away a pause and he drunk water. 'So far so good' acknowledged him that I am listening to his detailed scene description.

'Then next round was different; he had some different moves and was all over me. First time since my first tournament, my opponent was leading the score board. He was leading by 10 points after two rounds.'

'Wow, 10 points? Really? That's huge, he should have been brilliant to hit you ten times in the first place. If he was 10 points ahead, can only image his ability.'

'Yes, he was very good. Something happened to me seeing him move 10 points ahead. Blood was pumping at a rate faster than a bullet train. Went at him full force, no holding back. I gave him serious of punches and after one of my mighty right-hand punches, thought he won't get up again. Within the count of two he stood on his feet. He can take a hard hit and he has lot of heart and seriously a good fighter. In the fourth round beginning itself he dominated me. I had less reply to his swift moves. Then, hell broke out of me. Something just pumped inside, one minute fiercely punched him with all my strength, wasn't even looking at where I was punching. I can feel my hands and muscles are completely out of my control. I was gaining speed and points also went above him. By the time my rage was over, he falls down unconscious.'

'I hardly noticed that I had beaten down a boy to death. I was so proud of myself moving towards my side of the ring. The rage and fierce made me feel like an animal. He lost lot of blood and admitted to ICU ward. I was no help to him, unable to give my blood, different blood groups.'

'So, you decided to stay near him until he recovers fully?'

'Decided to stay to make sure I won't hurt another person like this ever again.'

'Sure, our sports master was furious about it.' We both got up on our way to class room.

'Yes, he tried to console me and advised me lot. I ignored to listen his any practicality or old ancient wisdom. So, openly ignored his speech. He was upset and he also knew about my stubbornness, so went along.'

'Anyone in his family scolded you?'

'They were all kind to me. Even his sister, who was couple of years older than me, tried to console me while crying.'

'You are too emotional and sensitive, you know that?'

'For a good reason I guess.' We walked little briskly towards the class.

'So, full stop for boxing?'

'Full stop for fighting. I am done with it.' Stern noise denoting its purpose.

'You are the one to tell never take decision on impulse. Now I guess you are taking it in a hurry. You have passion for fighting and you are really good at this.'

'I have a passion for challenge. At the same time, I don't want to hurt anyone, especially the good ones. This is a well thought out clear and correct decision for me and others.'

'I still feel you are taking a decision in emotion. I just hope you change.'

'Good or Bad, Right or Wrong, I own my decision. I never have regrets, Akhil. If wrong or incorrect, will learn from it. It is inevitable you will make a wrong decision at some point in life. But the decision is mine, taken on my own. That freedom I want to always have with me. It's better to be wrong.'

Put my arms around his shoulder 'Punch line at last, that's my friend. Now you are really talking.' We both chuckled, entered the class room, and took our seat.

From next day he quit mixed martial arts training and fighting skills he was learning. Our sports master was disappointed, yet he redirected him to cricket and athletics coach. Last year itself he was giving less importance to these two sports activities at school. Both he likes very much as it presents what he expects, a challenge.

He didn't take part in any of these sports. I wondered why he is ruing such a gift. When I enquired about it, he simply said he lost interest in these things. I strongly felt something more to it than what he revealed. The detective in me searched for reasons from various quarters in school.

I was unable to crack the entire story. From trusted sources, the information I got is there is too much of corruption, fraud, and politics in these two categories of sports in our school. Couple of times Abbay tried to stay away from inappropriate things, but they were forcing him to lie and support terrible things. He is never going to accept for such things even if his life was at stake.

He gave deep thoughts on acquiring his sponsorship money by some other means now. He was looking for part time job at somewhere to ensure less burden for his father. The martial arts master was so keen in keeping Abbay and training him. He offered him to help in others practise and responsibility of collecting fee and maintaining the account. Abbay is honest and truthful. He has amazing fighting skills, a gifted one as per the master. The martial arts master offered Abbay exactly what he needed.

He took that part time job. In week days every day morning one hour and evening two hours. Saturday and Sunday morning four hours were his job timing. He got a good amount of money every month, unlike one-time huge amount that he got a prize or gift. He was earning by himself with a solid job at the age of fourteen.

In the ninth standard, we were very serious about studies. Abbay was the same as he was in the previous years. He persisted to avoid use vulgar words and *"Site seeing"* – watching girls, following them, flirting, or abusing them. Other boys neglected him as the fear has gone away.

Chapter 15 – Career Decision

Abbay also remained at his place, mostly talking or spending time with me and Naren in the class. I found some of the things are very interesting about girls the way other boys talked, I really wanted to join them because they justified it is hormone change and very natural. Then I knew, Abbay will be right about things. So, put my faith in my best friend and was hiding my true feeling.

The discussion about my future was prime scene at home every day. Dad wanted me to become a software engineer. He even went one step ahead and bought a new desktop computer to motivate me. I wasn't really into it or anybody in my family. The only person who liked this new device was Anjali. She spends a lot of time in it and was good in operating the machine.

Next my mom, who wanted me to become a doctor. She wanted me to become a heart surgeon as Keerthi wished to become. When she talks about doctor, I still feel some unusual disturbance in my stomach due to the big syringe. She was trying her way to inspire me.

I felt two careers are tricky. In fact, I never had a goal or aim. The confusion was too big for me to resolve of my own. At children's park when Anjali and Keerthi were looking after smaller kids, sat never Abbay.

'Do you have any goal or aim?'

'Hmm.... Like becoming a heart surgeon?'

'Yes' expecting a satisfactory answer from him. Any field he is going to say, I am going to do the same.

'I am unlikely to plan that far ahead. I will take my career that is challenging and I am passionate and enjoying type.' His clear answer only made me feel disappointed.

'How will you find out which field you will enjoy and passionate about?' trying on search for some relative answer.

'From my understanding, if you have passion for it, nothing will stop you until you figure out or finish. Sleep, food or any other will become trivial. Only the passionate thing will become the most important thing for you.'

This gave me an idea to look forward. Certainly not computer or any electronics or mechanical device. My dad says many types of engineering are there to figure out which suits you more. When refit loose cycle chain or use screw to open table fan and clean, dad will encourage me to become mechanical engineer. I have decided to take my own passion. Follow his idea and hope I will find my passion.

Our science teacher was extremely skilful and possess in depth knowledge in biology. He was very descriptive and explained in detail. The classes were interesting and most of us listened to him. There was one lesson in our school book about human reproductive system. Many of us so eagerly awaited the day he is going to take that lesson.

Our science teacher explanation was very short, within 15 minutes he might have completed the entire lesson. It was like he purposefully did that. In other higher classes too, they only touched a bit on this topic and no one explained in detail. When enquired about it came to know that many years ago one of the girls in the class complained about the teacher for explaining reproductive system in the class, mentioning it was very vulgar. From that day no teacher talks about it in detail.

Now I got more interest to read it, just because of the curiosity to know what was in it. First read the lesson and tried to understand the concepts. Many words are new for me and needed a dictionary to know the meaning first. As I started to learn few things, very unusual things were happening in my body. I felt it very odd and extremely strange.

It was a Saturday morning, after breakfast got into my room and read the lesson again to understand it clearly. Three hours of full concentration, was learning things and on each passing moment my interest doubled. Mom forced me to get out for lunch.

After lunch, logged into the computer and my first actual search on google. Our book was less descriptive to understand the whole concept. So, looking for more resources to learn sounded like a logical choice to me. Evening avoided playing and went to nearby library to get some book names that I found in google.

The books were for doctors. Again, unfamiliar words and dictionary became necessary. I was wake till 4 AM in the morning, kept on reading books. I fell asleep unknowingly at some point. The next day morning, realized I found my passion and happily informed my mom that I am going to become a doctor.

There are many human parts which got my eye. But, after some time I figured out how it works and remedy measures in book, it was less fascinating.

The most interesting chapter was about brain and nervous system. I felt it is the most complicated part and by keep digging in, learnt there is very less people who are specialists related to these categories.

Finally, I decided what I should become, a neurologist. My research work on various human parts continued, now limited myself to take care of health as one of books suggested to have perfect balance in life.

The tenth standard is very important as the marks we get in public examination will let us decide what career we can choose. I was confident to take Biology as my major subject in 11th and 12th standard. For this, I need to get more than 90 % in annual public exam. Getting the required percentage is not going to be a big deal for me, a piece of cake.

Chapter 16 – Turnaround

Everything was going perfect and much to my surprise, Abbay and Keerthi were no longer having silly fights and both acted more mature. Now they are very good friends and have better understanding.

Maximum a week might have passed in the school, tides turned and Abbay's smooth sailing life came to halt. He was at school and around 2 PM the clerk came to class. Teacher and clerk spoke with him for a couple of minutes. He was looking down to the bench and took his bag. I can see tears on his eyes. He does not want to look at anyone of us.

We were curious on what happened and the first thing I did is go to his home as soon as school was over. A huge crowd gathered, more confusion and fear surrounded me. Gone through the big crowd and went near the gate. His parents were in two ice boxes with yellow flowers all over the box. Anjali was hugging him and crying. He was also crying looking at his parent's dead body in a complete disbelief.

I stood stunned unable to react or do anything. My mom came near me and took inside the house. She explained that both lost their life in a road accident. They died on the spot as the injury was on the head. I was still trying to stabilize and unable to image what has happened.

I had no idea on what to say to Abbay. How can I possibly console him? After few minutes went towards dad and openly asked what should I tell Abbay. He advised me better to leave him alone and after few days he believed things will come back to normal.

Without knowing what to do I stayed around the corner and was looking at Abbay. He was trying not to cry; assume for the past two hours he has been crying. Anjali was exhausted and rested her head on his shoulder, looking at her parents. Keerthi came there and screamed. They were as much as parents for her too.

Unable to control myself, went to rest room and cried. The happiest family on earth with only good thoughts and good things among them, why should suffer like this? Why did God had taken their life this quickly? What will happen to Abbay and Anjali? How these two are going to survive?

All questions came to my mind. When I came out the rest room, only able to hear Abbay's parent's laughter. Came to my home for dress change. I remained outside and Abbay went to do the final rituals as per their customs. His head was full shaved as per their religious belief.

The thought of losing parents haunted me. I will be nothing without them.

After couple of days, came to know that, his uncle and aunt will be legal guardian for him and Anjali. It was a good deal for them. They have two children and his uncle was only a taxi driver whose earnings are less. They don't have their own home or money. Abbay parent's property and savings came handy for them.

They moved here with entire family and now, Abbay and Anjali must live them. I was shuddered by the thought of living with uncle and aunt. The suffering and things that Keerthi went through still haunts me. What if the same happens for Abbay and Anjali? It's impossible to hurt Anjali when he is around, what happens when he is not with her? The questions were raising inside me, without any answers.

During weekend, went to Abbay's home looking for him. In the room, Abbay was sitting on the cot and Anjali was sleeping resting her head on his thigh. He greeted me to come inside, for a while I sat there. He was in no mood to talk and I felt uneasy. Almost sat there for an hour without speaking anything.

Lunch time came and I was back to my home. They both are in grief and powerless to move on. His house was very small. Only single bed room, a hall, and a kitchen. The reason I went there was to look whether my friend got proper attention by his uncle's family. It seemed normal to me. They are sleeping in the hall. Abbay and Anjali were using the only available room, which gave me proof that things are good so far.

The next week Sunday around 3 PM, Keerthi came to my home. She asked me to come to sphere ground as Abbay was sitting alone under the tree. I was reading about digestive system, without a second thought raced towards Sphere ground. Abbay already had the company of Naren and Nirmal.

We both sat near him, as usual I sat next to him. There was a grim silence for some time. Then it was Keerthi to start off. 'How is Anjali?'

'She is fine.' Abbay said very mildly.

Keerthi knew, he isn't going to say much so prepared to launch more questions. 'Is she mingling well with your uncle's family?'

'No.' Abbay indicated expectation to stop talking.

'Your aunt is treating you guys well?'

'So far, good.' He was keeping it real short.

'Are you okay?' She is unsatisfied with three words reply, she wants him to talk.

Abbay turned his head around towards Keerthi and chortled. 'Not really. Trying my level best to move on.' A better and lengthy reply from him.

She smiled back to him as she liked that large answer. Only she was talking, we three boys still unsure on how to talk with him. After a minute again Keerthi said, 'It will be impossible for Anjali to move, if you don't. You are the only person she trusts and you are her world now.'

'Yes, that's true. She never leaves my side. Always sad and never talks with anyone else. She is not even having her food properly. Uncle and aunt both are nice and understanding her grief, they are going easy on her.' Abbay understood unless Keerthi gets what she wants, she is going to keep on bugging, so gave answer all she is looking for.

'That's great to hear. Keep an eye on your aunt to make sure your sister is unharmed.' Keerthi threw caution to the wind.

'Yes, know all about your aunt. Our situation is same, as once it was for you. I am careful, but I am not judging or fixing any thought on aunt. She is a good person.'

'Yes, she speaks with me nicely. Why did she asked for home and claimed your parent's insurance money and used for her kids?' Keerthi was suspicious and the point looked valid to us three. We looked at each other and thought of entering the discussion.

'It was a practical choice. Uncle is earning less and they have two kids. No house on their own. Now, they don't need to pay rent here, the debts are off with insurance amount. She has invested the remaining amount in gold and bank deposits to secure future for her children. Something that any mother would do. If she is cruel, she might have thrown us out or treat us badly. She is treating Anjali like her own daughter. I don't think she is going to be a rogue.' He was sure and clear on his thoughts.

We accepted and so did Keerthi. She was throwing dice just to make him talk, we are tube light in understanding that, but we figured it out now.

Naren after a thought, 'Sure you miss your parents.'

'Yes, of course. I feel like there isn't anyone to take care of me or treat me special anymore.' His tone was grim and very soft.

'You have us' Naren quick to change his thoughts.

'I know, what I am saying is little different. Hope you understand.' Abbay back to where he started. Sure, we boys are very poor in dealing things in such situations.

'You are special to me. I may not able to take care of you all time, but I can be there for you and will be there for ever' I spoke to ensure Abbay feels light.

He chucked and put his hand on my shoulder. Keerthi knew that wasn't enough for him to move on.

She said, 'What exactly you feel you are missing?'

'Simply, the purpose. Feels like no one is there for me.' He persisted.

'It's not about whether you are loved or cared or treated special someone. Look at this way, you have someone to love, care and treat special. I think it's enough purpose. Anjali is there for you to taken care of.'

Keerthi thought was intriguing. Abbay got sense out of it someone.

'How did you got over, when your parents died? Or tortured by your aunt?' He put a critical question.

'I never saw my parents. So, never knew how it feels when someone cares for you. I am unlike you, neither too emotional nor too sensitive. I have a huge desire to live and go to certain highs in life, enjoy and acquire every good thing about life. So, that drove me. When I received thrashing and bleeding, one occasion thought of better to die than live with pain. It was a little kitten hobbling around my legs that changed my mind. I would say she was the reason. We all have and will always have someone to look over and take care, if we look for. Now see how many are there to take care of me? I have many parents now.'

Abbay chuckled. 'Of all, I never thought you will make me feel better.'

'I am just different, very different compared to you.' Keerthi was laughing out loud.

'Ok, all. I am leaving for gym. It's been two weeks since I went there. Have to start fee collection from tomorrow, going to check with master.'

It was very refreshing to see Abbay back like this. He had already planned to go. He knew we would come and make him feel better. And he was very right, of all we never thought that Keerthi is going to speak good and make him feel better. It was a pleasant surprise to us.

Keerthi stayed with us for a while and came with me to my home. On the way there was an element in the kitten story that was bothering me for a while.

'You made that kitten story, don't you?' I asked her to make sure my intentions are clear, that I am going to tease her at some point.

'Kind of. When I felt bad, the kitten used to change my mood. Just decorated a few things around. I know very well about Abbay. When his father used to tell him any ancient wisdom or some philosophy, his father will tell with an underlying story and he will listen carefully. I was just using the same idea.'

'Whatever!! But the story was melodramatic and piece of shit.' Got the right opportunity to tease her.

Her smiling face shrunk. 'Anyway, it worked.'

'Yes, only he would have listened to that.'

We were near the gate and she came in front me. She got the hold of the gate and chortled. 'You are jealous of me!'

'For what? Telling the worst story ever?' I got under her skin now.

'Yes, you are. For knowing your friend better and able to change his mood, manipulate, brain washed and done the impossible – *to outsmart Abbay!*' She was very proud of herself.

'You outsmarted "*The Abbay?*" In your dreams. He does things in his own way. If you think you had outsmarted him, means he wanted to create that delusion. You know him better than me? He was already planning to go to gym, he came and sat at Sphere ground so that you will come and he can relax. You fool, you never outsmarted him. He used you to make him feel better.'

Now she is depressed. 'But, I came and called you guys?' She was curious to figure out.

'If Abbay want to meet me or others, he will directly come to our home and call us. Else, he might have waited in the sphere little longer, he knew we will come to play cricket anyway. He came and sat there when no one was around, so that he can have a conversation with you. He knew you will definitely tell something that will cheer him up.'

She now realized the logic on my speech. She stood stun at the gate while I went inside. I dropped my foot-wear and ready to move. Turned around and got ready to make a final dig at her.

'You know, Abbay baba used to tell an ancient punch line. "*A foolish cat closed its eye and thought that the world has become dark. Many people are also like that, thinking they are known it all, genius! And everything in the world happens on their action.*" I must confess he is right and had seen one now' Had a cunning smile on my face.

She got furious 'You.... I am going to kill you!' She screamed and chased me to beat. I went right into the kitchen near mom and Keerthi must remain good girl.

Things are moving on very fast. Anjali is going to school with her cousin sister and it's only me and Abbay now. I liked it very much because we are having lot of discussion while riding in cycle on the way and back from school. Abbay now got complete trust in his aunt and he is leaving Anjali with them. She too mingled with them. She used to spend a lot of time in computer and kitchen with my mom.

Abbay was getting along with regular routines, going to gym and evening cricket at the ground. He didn't want to become captain of the cricket team as many of them playing with us are college or working persons. Everyone saw great leadership quality in him and they forced him to take it.

Abbay was ruthless with ball in hand. His way of captaining was very different. More closing and attacking field settings. He insisted team members to look for wickets all the time irrespective of score or position. He could turn some games we are about to lose to victory simply by the approach.

We were almost unbeatable. In the past six months, we might have lost only three or four matches. We won all the remaining. Our team named as "*Silent Assassins*" after the way Abbay does things. He is very popular among everyone because of the knowledge, tactics, and techniques he uses on the field.

He wasn't getting the same respect at school. As he is trying to avoid brawls, some boys took it as advantage. They provoked him for fight many times using harsh words, teasing him and even they went such an extend to tease Anjali. He tried his level best to avoid or ignore them.

If Nirmal, Naren or I was there, we will stand up for Abbay. Nirmal is always ready to fight and some boys received lashes from him for over doing with Abbay. He is not as strong or skilful as Abbay, but he too knows karate and mixed martial arts as he followed Abbay's footsteps.

Nirmal always used to tell Abbay to avoid letting them go at you and punish them. He was hundred percent sure that none of them can bear a single punch from Abbay. Abbay gave big lectures and philosophies on why he keeps moving away from fights. Nirmal after hearing all this will persist with his approach. *"He is the mighty sun - Abbay and they are like ants"* Abbay corrected him that are barking dogs. Dogs bark at Sun, but the Sun is invincible and always remain beyond the reach of dogs.

Nirmal really liked this thought and whenever anyone tried to provoke Abbay, he will say what Abbay said, every time in different insulting manner.

Chapter 17 – The Second Strike

Even at the gym, they didn't leave Abbay to live in peace. They all thought because of joining there, we are supporting Abbay. The fools thought process were less, we are also practising the same fights for more than 6 years. None us is any match to Abbay strength or skills or stamina.

The martial arts master will always be there to avoid any fights and if you get into one, he will throw you out of the gym from the next day. When Abbay collects fee, they will try to insult him but, he smartly traders the insult back at them.

There was big talk in our colony about goons and fight at the gym. I was little scared for Abbay and went to his home. He was asleep and it is unusual for Abbay to sleep in the afternoon. I decided to stay and sat next to him and begin to read a book.

After some time, Abbay woke up and he suggested to go to ground. He was very silent on the way to ground. Keerthi was already sitting under the big tree. Naren and Nirmal was not there, so I assumed, they knew. Abbay was checking with Keerthi about her sponsor.

Abbay in a disappointed voice, "The master is going to shut down the gym and move to other state. I have to find a new part time job."

'What happened there, yesterday?' I wasted no time and straight into the point.

'There has been some problem with goons for couple of weeks. They were asking money from the martial arts master for letting him have the gym. He had the legal documents and so he didn't oblige. They were giving trouble to master at home. He filed a complaint against them in police. When police went to investigate goons, they beat them and brought injured police to the gym.'

Keerthi jolted by the events Abbay describing her. She interrupted his flow 'You are there when those goons came?' shuddered Keerthi asked like she is shivering.

Abbay nodded his head. 'Yes. Our master tried not to indulge in fight. But the goons beat the boys practising. One of the constables told master to run and save himself and other students. While, the other said to beat these rascals and he will ensure that mater will not have any trouble.'

Suddenly my fear is gone and now curious to know the about what happened. If Abbay is here, sure might have beaten then so hard that they might have never again think of even looking at the master. Keerthi was more worried now.

'Master fought with them?' She hoped that Abbay remained at bay.

'Master asked us to run and we all obeyed him. The goons had weapons in their hand and threaten to hurt the students. Master knew there is no way out and he asked for fight alone with him and not to trouble any of his students.'

'The goons agreed to the deal, master asked me to take all the students out. I tried to take them out and but many of the guys were scared to leave master alone, because there were more than fifteen goons.'

Keerthi again interrupted, 'You too stayed there?' Again, he nodded his head. By now I got irritated and almost yelled at her 'Will you let him speak and finish it?' She nodded head and looked at Abbay to listen.

'One of the guys hit with a big rod on master's head from behind. Master was not expecting it as they were still talking. Still, he measured the swing and tried to move away. The rod hit him in the fore head instead of a knock in the back head. He was bleeding, got up and kicked that guy fiercely. All other goons surrounded and threw weapons at him.'

He gave a little break. Keerthi was about to ask a question, saw me with raised eye brow and slant head. She understood, I wanted her to listen to him without disturbing.

'Then, I knew master couldn't handle all of them by himself. So, joined him and helped him.' He simply finished and looked at both.

'You fought with the goons?' She was furious of what he did.

'Yes, we beat them and police constables took them to hospital. They ensured us that they will close the case as they beat the goons and we are out of trouble. Today master and his family decided to switch place to avoid further trouble.'

'What? They are leaving the place putting all of you boys in trouble? You guys fought for him, he should stay and face any further trouble.' From being shivering in fear, now she got angry.

'Master is still in hospital, unconscious. The decision was made by their family, which I believe is the right choice.' He so eloquently said the reality.

'You hadn't thought of the worst part. You all little boys involved in fight with goons. They might have a big gang and come for you. I had experience on this, trust me! The police will not help in this. I had faced.' Keerthi was over reacting and she always prepare for the worst, anything less than worst will make her feel good. I won't blame her for it, after all she has gone through.

'Never come into conclusion about people, Keerthi. I have told you many times to try to think positive and trust at least few in life. The police had already helped us in this. Sekhar also works in the police department. If any problem arrives, I will seek his help. Ok? Stop thinking too much and worrying. I am going to be fine.' He maintained the pitch as soft as he can.

'Just be more careful Abbay.' She spoke. He nodded his head and looked at the team gathering.

'Hey, they all want to know happened. I think you may need to tell the same story to them as well. I will leave it up to you. Once, we start playing I will join you guys.' I said to Abbay and he moved.

I felt Abbay is not telling the whole thing as it happened. Too many lose ends. They both fought, master is injured unconscious at the hospital, things didn't add up. I am sure Abbay won't discuss with us any further on it. So, decided to wait for Nirmal and Naren to come.

Keerthi was about to leave for home, she waited a second and asked me, 'You are waiting for someone?'

'Yes, I want to hear the actual story from Naren and Nirmal.' I was giving hand signals to Naren to come to me.

'Actual story? You think it is story? You think Abbay will lie to us?' Keerthi was little confused on what I am looking for.

'No, He will never lie to anyone. "*Story*" is just a kidding phrase. He has told it very simple and easy. I want to know elaborate detailed scene description.' I was still trying to get Naren's attention.

Keerthi came back and sat next to me. She was also curious to know the detail. 'Naren won't help you much in knowing the detail. He is same as Abbay in keeping things simple on things like this.'

'Yes, that's right. Nirmal will definitely come along with Naren.' I was confident in what I am doing.

As expected, both Naren and Nirmal came. We told them what we know so far. I asked them what exactly happened.

'As Abbay said they fought and over thrown the attackers. Because of head injury master was down unconscious and admitted to hospital. If he was serious Abbay would be with him.' Naren just cut off the discussion and about to leave.

'No, Akhil. Abbay only told the intro of fight. It was something else, beyond one's imagination. Wow, unbelievable. The way he moved and thrashed those goons' Nirmal was quick to tell.

'Only Abbay fought with the goons?' I was getting the picture of what happened.

Before Nirmal is going to open his mouth, Naren interrupted, 'Me and Abbay both said the truth. If you want to hear any melodramatic movie like script, you can listen to this idiot.' He ran towards the team without further taking part in the discussion.

'Why he is so harsh? I am going to just tell exactly what happened.' Nirmal looking at his twin in disarray.

Keerthi quick to jump on and curious to know 'Leave him, Nirmal. Your brother spent too much with time with Abbay, him and Akhil are becoming same as Abbay.' I looked at her from top to bottom. She signed by shrinking her cute eyes to let me know that she said to provoke Nirmal to talk and that what happened.

'Yes, that's correct. My mom told me today to keep distance from Abbay. Everybody fears him now.' Nirmal with lot of mixed expressions and emotions within a single sentence.

'Ok, Nirmal. Tell us now.' I desperately wanted the details.

'Master fought well at the beginning. But when two big guys close to 7 feet tall grabbed and punched, he fell and lot of blood sprayed. Abbay ran towards master and lifted him up. He gave a daring look. We are able to hear his muscle gripping sound and he stood like...'

'Ok, we understand that. Assume you are planning the movie script that you are about to write. It's great and poetic. Unfortunately, we are less imaginary than you. So, just tell us in simple and easy language.' I wanted to avoid his extravagant gossips.

'You are right Keerthi. Akhil too has changed.' He passed to take a deep breath.

'Abbay moved like air, flying around the men with dangerous weapons in their hand. One punch for one goon and they hardly got back on the feet. The seven-foot-tall raised his big wall like arms to punch Abbay. Abbay punched right into his hands. We can hear the both finger bones crushing. The big guy's bone broke from wrist to shoulder, we could see the shoulder bone came out of skin. All other goons stood shunned for a minute.'

'Ok, that's great description. Can we skip on a little bit and move to the end?' I almost told him to shut the non-sense and finish it.

Disappointed Nirmal, 'Then what, he took barely more than a minute to take all seventeen goons on his own. Nobody else in the gym moved an inch and all boys looked stunned. Especially our class boys who used to tease him, they were afraid as if they saw the ghost on move. He was lighting quick and at his best. Though he is not fighting, he still possesses all the skills and strength. Everyone frightened to see him, including the police constables. When he asked them to take those thugs, they saluted him and said "*Yes, Sir.*"'

'Abbay beat all seventeen of them in a minute?' Keerthi felt the fear of facing him.

'Maybe he took a couple of minutes. But, no one can guess how much time he took, because the fight was over before we even realized the war was begun.'

'Abbay said the goons are in hospital. He beat them that hard in couple of minutes?' Her fear is beyond reach now.

'One more hit he would have killed them. He was very careful only in hurting and ensuring they remain alive. If he wanted, he might have done that with a single punch itself. I guess he doesn't want to spend rest of his life in jail. That's why he went little easy on those thugs.' Nirmal elaborated the correct fact about fight at last.

Keerthi was at complete disbelieve and turned towards me with her mouth wide open.

'What? Close your mouth first?' I teased her right away. She closed her mouth and looked clueless at me.

'What are you thinking of Abbay, Keerthi? I have told you many times, he can take on anybody in this world. Ten or fifteen, even it was fifty goons, he might have thrashed them with ease. Those muscles and fighting skills are result of years of practise sessions. From birth he stretched, strengthened his muscle and no one can beat him unless he wants to be beaten.' I was trying to explain about my dear friend's capacity to her.

Nirmal was nodding his head in acknowledgement. Keerthi was regrouping herself. 'Then why did he let those stupid boys tease him? One punch might be enough' She yelled at us more in disbelief.

'One punch might be enough to what? Kill a teenage boy, who studied with you in the same class for five years? Break his bones and let his mom/dad help him to eat, use restroom and cry every day on their boy's condition?' I too yelled back at her stating the reality of the situation.

Her head was down and we all were silent for a moment. 'What about those thugs at the hospital? What will happen if they wanted revenge?' She is a very strange and fearful girl.

Nirmal and me both laughed. Nirmal went on 'I think they will never be able to use their legs or hands in the same way as before. They are from other state as police said, so I think it is better for them to stay away from Abbay. He will crush them if they want revenge or anything like that.'

'You guys are describing like old movie hero. Any action done at an impulse will haunt you forever in life.' She never backs off from her thoughts.

'Abbay never does anything on impulse. He should have been forced to the extreme to act violently. He knows the consequence of fighting at that situation. He knows very well how to handle if they ever want to take revenge. I understand you care for him. Stop making it so big deal. And rightly said, this isn't a movie, he isn't a hero. You are the one should think practically. Practically the goons can't dominate like invincible Dons as shown in the movies. You get into reality. It was fight and he saved others from the bad guys. That's it.' That was probably the longest explanation I had given to anybody till that day.

Finally, she decided to let it go and we were off to play cricket. Master and his family member vacated the home. Abbay now became jobless. He started looking for it and got couple of offers from hotels as waiter and delivery boy. If it was his parents, he might have convinced them. His uncle and aunt rejected it. They are completely against part time jobs, especially like this.

Abbay obeyed their words, because now they are more of his family. They treated both Abbay and Anjali very well like their own children. Abbay liked them very much and if you are close to him, he doesn't mind adjusting or doing things for you.

Chapter 18 – Strange Goals

10th standard annual public exams are only away by a month. Many students scared and stressed out to get good marks. Anything less than 90% is average score. Everyone had book in their hands all the time.

At home I got some special treatment from my parents. When I studied late night, they will be awake for me. Mom will at least twice ask me for coffee or fresh juice. It always makes you feel good irrespective of how old you get when someone care for you. I liked all these things.

Parents of other students now cut TV cable connection and blocked satellite channels. They stopped their kids from going to playground. They were doing all crazy things to make their child study hard.

There was no such trouble for me. Mom and dad never restricted me playing or any other activities. I know my responsibilities and will always spend adequate time to study. My parents trusted me and as I was knocking the first rank with ease. I only got new gifts from them.

I completely forgot to give a thought on Abbay. Since, gym is no more, he will have plenty of time now to study and do other things. He was spending more time at playground in the evening and works out in the morning.

One Sunday evening when I was studying physics interestingly, mom and Keerthi asked me about Abbay and what's his plan. Then only I came to realize how casual he is taking these exams.

They both went back to kitchen. I was restless and I know Abbay will be at the ground. I informed mom and she knew I was going to do that. She smiled at me gracefully. He was already in the middle of the match and I joined team.

We are ready to go home. I went towards park and sat on the bench. Abbay came with me and we both liked the pleasant breeze.

'What you are doing on normal days?'

'Coming to school, of course.' Abbay laughed and spinning the ball in his hands.

I saw him with irritation. 'What are you doing on the leisure time in the morning and in the evening?'

'I was searching for job that is descent and study related so that uncle and aunt will accept me to go.'

'Any success there?'

'None. Will find it soon. I don't want to be a burden for them. I want to help them financially. Have some saving that will help me in paying first term for next year. After that have to get pocket money from them. I want to be on my own, earn my own money for everything.'

'It's a good attitude. Are you forgetting about the most immediate problem? The 10th annual exams?'

'I will crack 80%, which I think should be enough.' Abbay casually throwing the ball high up in the air and catching.

'80% is now considered as only average mark. You must get above 90% if you are going to have better future.'

'I have no interest or passion like you. I just want challenge and adventure in life. Your ideology won't suit my case.'

'You are the one who helped me in finding my passion. Now, I want to become a neurologist due to our idea.'

He chuckled. 'So, now what you are going to payback?'

'No, I am trying to understand what you want with life. What do you want to become?'

'I am not going to become, anything or anybody. I am going to enjoy my life that is going to full of thrill and adventure.'

'Ok, fair enough. How exactly are you going to achieve?'

'I searched a bit and asked opinions. I think I got basically four options, 1. Documenting wild life, 2. Documenting extreme weather conditions, 3. Research on climate and life forms in Arctic and Antarctic regions, 4. Travel to space – I would love to have an inter galactic travel'

'I think you need to have certain knowledge to work on any of these fields. Gave a thought for it?' His goals and dreams surprised me a lot. Then, he is a clear guy and knows exactly what he is doing. So, tried to know what he had figured out so far.

'I want to do all first three things. I am learning a little bit on photography. This will help in doing them. Fourth mighty be light difficult. Haven't given upon it yet, reading Astro-nuclear-physics whenever I feel like learning it.'

'So, first you will become wild life photographer. Once you start feeling it is boring, you will be camera man for some channel covering extreme weather conditions. Then, go to polar regions and research on ice? Wow, that's some goal' I chortled sensing it is highly impossible.

'I know it sounds crazy and an impossible day dream. I would like to do them all, including space travel.'

'Nothing is impossible for you, that one thing I am most certain about. I just feel it is too much to do in a single life time. I know you had already done the thought process for it and going towards achieving them.'

'Yes, it is too much. But, let's say I got enough fun and thrill in wild life photography, I might stick with it for my life time. Only if I get bored, I have to look for another adventure.'

His plan was clear and I felt no need to worry about his future. He is searching for a job related to photography which is his first step towards the target.

'Ok, you have a good plan and you know what's the next step. Now, for me score more than 90%. Just more than 90%, all you need to do is spend couple of more hours before exam I guess.'

'Hmm... Anjali said the same thing. Keerthi gave long advise to score 98% and get state first. She is motivating that I have capability and blah blah blah... Ok, I will get more than 90 in all subjects, you have my word on it.'

'Your word is all that matters to me.' I knew it for sure, he will keep his word irrespective of what happens.

'Now, shall we leave?' Abbay asked as if he wants something.

'Let's race towards my home!' I said and started running straightway. Abbay is having bat and ball in his hands, so took the advantage. Unfortunately, he beat me to the gate. We both were laughing, he me the bat and left for his home.

The public exam was in progress, after exam everyone was searching and discussing whether the answers, they wrote were correct. I really felt for some of the students who found that they had given some wrong answers. They looked depressed and jolted. Thankfully for us Abbay decided to not do this by 6th standard itself and we were all following him.

Abbay was still casual as he went for half an hour jogging at the ground every morning. Even on exam days, he used to do the same. My mom and dad were very unpleasant of this behaviour and they even talked about it with him. He was just acknowledging them with respect, he continued his own ways.

Exams were over and summer holidays arrived. It was a huge relief for all us. The tension and anxiety surrounded for last two months is finally gone. We are very happy and playing and chatting all the time.

Keerthi was on to something every serious. She was studying a lot and occasionally came out. I thought she is back to her sheath mode of avoiding boys. We are her only friends and so if she is avoiding us then there is some trouble for sure.

Abbay directly approached the orphan home's secretary. He was one of the friends of Abbay's father and hence he provided the information.

Keerthi didn't get money from her sponsor for last three months. There was letter from her sponsor stating to take care of her exam fee and next year's first term fees as there are problem with their current financial situation. She checked for other sponsors, but unable to get one.

Couple girls in the home dropped out of school last year due to insufficient funds. They are now working at home doing embroidery work, making toys, etc. Keerthi doesn't want to end up like them, she has a big dream which she is been running after, since her childhood.

I knew she was trying her luck with cross words and sudoku in newspapers for price money. She rarely got success. May be two or three times in the last two years. She sold some of her books, clothes and accessorises to manage exam fee. Now she is preparing for a quiz program and if she wins, she will get enough money for the first term fees.

When analogous situation rose a couple of years ago, she asked my parents and Abbay's parents for help. Abbay's parents gave money for exam fee and my parents took care of term fees. She might have asked this time too. Sure, my parents will be able to afford her term fee one time. If she is not doing there should be a reason. Abbay tried to talk with her but only got darts.

She was at my home. Mom and dad were asleep. I slowly moved towards her. She looked at me as I am coming near of some other intention.

'Hey, I heard about your term fees problem. You can ask mom and dad. They will sure help you.' Whispered in her ears ensuring other's sleep goes uninterrupted.

She was reading a book about population and economy. She closed it and smiled at me.

'No, Akhil. Your parents and Abbay's parents had done a lot for me. In fact, your parents are still helping me lot. I am spending more time at your home than at the orphanage. I don't want to make it difficult for any one.'

'Hey, this just one term fees. Probably for next term, you will get it from your sponsor again.'

'For past five years got lot of money from sponsor. They have taken care of all my needs school, books, bags, and uniform. From orphanage common share I got food and clothes. If they are having financial problem, it makes me feel bad. If they had saved the money spend for me, they might have evaded this crisis. Moreover, I want to be like Abbay. Look at him, he is earning for the past five years. He never wants to be in debt or owe anyone anything. He is person of pride and self-esteem. I want to be like him, take care of myself.'

I chuckled. 'Now, you too want to be like him ah? That's his speciality. '

'Who would want to live like hippy, looking for thrill and adventure? Just this quality I like in him.'

'Yes, that's how it will start. I don't want to force you. Remember we are always there to help you.' I moved towards the door to go out and she continued her reading.

A new arrival of family nearby to our house. They were from some other state I believe. There were five children in the family. In colony meeting, they informed that one of their girls has hallucination problem, so others should take on her carefully. She is here for treatment and once she gets well, they will be back to their homeland.

I know about this problem from my reading about brain. I was little curious to find out what this girl is like and study her. She looked perfectly normal. She behaved normally and was talking quite well with Keerthi. She is also of our same age. Her exam results came much before compared to us and she has secured 95% in the exams.

She is good in studies, speaks kindly, act normally and why people are saying she is abnormal? The question made me to research. Her father has huge belief in astrology and ghost. The gossip is that when Nancy (*the girl with hallucinations*) was 4 years old, ghost attacked and possessed her. Even after all these years of exorcism, it still haunts her.

The day came when she acted abnormally, it was a full moon day as they predicted. Her father and brother took her forcefully. The rumour is that they will chain her in the attic as in some movies.

It confused me. I was unsure whether to believe in ghost or not. I am a strong believer in God, ghost is probably very new one for me. Instead of looking for books about hallucinations, turned towards ghost. Some of the theory sounded logical to me about light and dark, good, and evil. If God exists, so does demon ghost.

The interesting think though is she is getting exorcism and treatment for hallucinations. I met her treatment doctor and leant a few things about her. According to him, this delusion of ghost inserted into her mind at a very young age by none other than her parents. Since, she was very little this cemented strong in her memory and she still think of attacked by ghost regularly. She is getting counselling from the doctor to remove that thought.

It was extremely difficult reaching the doctor or getting information from him. I did some mischiefs to get what I wanted. I decided to sit on the bay at this matter. Digging further felt problematic as I was little scared what if the ghost stories are true. Some of the ghost movie I saw that period was very scary and it played a huge part in making this decision.

I am not Abbay to walk fearless as a four-year-old kid around the graveyard. That's him and only he can be like that. He though never believes in all these things. Every kid and adult in the colony preferred to maintained distance from Nancy. After the full moon day incident Keerthi stayed away from her.

Many times, I felt pity for Nancy, as she sat alone in the park without any one next to her. Abbay tried couple of times to talk with her and help. Their parents now almost put her to house arrest. He voiced against brutally treating her in the name of exorcism and tried to make them stop it. He was unable to change their mindset and after couple of tries he let it go as fighting against every person's belief is not going to work.

Chapter 19 – Difficult Choice

Exam results came. I got 97% percentage, school first, district first and state fourth. My school sponsored the fees for the next two years to study. It was a day of celebrations for me and all of us. Abbay rejoiced my success and he got school third with 94.6%.

It was party time for all of us, but Keerthi was having a false smile. She got overall fourth in our school with 94.2%. If had she got third, the prize money will worth half of the first term fee amount. She was sad because she might have to discontinue her studies.

Abbay almost got all the needed money for his next term fees by securing 100 in maths. Only 26 students in the state got it and he is the only one to get in our school. We are applying for higher studies courses. I got biology and everyone applied.

To my surprise Keerthi was happy and she was filling application form. Abbay has given 75% of his price money to her. The remaining of course goes to help family. She now needs a very small vague for first term and she is very sure with her quiz competition victory.

Most of my class mates came and applied for higher studies. I waited till lunch to see Abbay. After that left with dad. I was disappointed and thinking what Abbay has planned to do.

Evening we met at the ground and I was furious at him. 'Why you are not there at school for applying?'

'Calm down, we will sit and discuss in detail.' Abbay understood my displeasure with him irrespective of anything he is going to say.

'I have already told you my plans, remember?' We sat under the tree. I looked at him angrily.

'So, what? You are going to stop studying and take a camera, go behind wild animals?' The volume at which I spoke showed the frustration.

'Yes. That's right. I am going to exactly do that.' Abbay nodding his head, moved his hands towards the pant pocket. He took a postal cover letter.

It was from some television program company for the post of assistant cameraman.

'This is illegal. You are below 18 years and for wild life cameraman you must be above 18 years. I will complain.' The frustration came out and I was unable to hold on to myself, didn't know what I was talking.

'Akhil, calm down. I know it is shock. Think practically. I want to go for several reasons and it is the best thing to do for me and everyone else. Also, I will earn and do what I like, every day will be an adventure.' Abbay graciously said that.

'Yes, adventure!! Eaten by lion, teared apart by tiger? Yes, that's fascinating.' I lost control of myself.

'If you listen to me, I will tell everything. Can you please?'

I turned away and gave the cover back to him. He slowly said, 'I told uncle and aunt few days before and convinced them this the best option financially as next year Anjali's fee will also be high. It was difficult to convince Anjali, she cried all day when the result came. Today I convinced her. So, all good.'

'" *Financial*"? that's what you told to convince uncle and aunt? Ok, how much are you going to earn?'

'Monthly 3000 rupees plus travel allowance.'

'Wow, that's huge amount of money. Well, done! That won't be enough for you to eat itself, lousy eater.' I really wanted to scold him in harsh words, controlled myself.

He is throwing way a wonderful opportunity, he has secured great marks and yet he is throwing away everything. More, I was angry because he is going to leave me and I won't be able to spend time with him.

'I am going to go inside deep forest. Our first project is 6 months tracking tigers and elephants, documenting their survival. In forest if you want to eat, you hunt, for shelter stay under a tree and I need basically 7 sets of clothes - *I think I have more than that*. All my income and travel allowance will be for my family and Anjali can get new clothes, buy gadgets, a computer and so on.'

Slowly it made sense to me. My anger is yet to go down and but, started to think. 'You said several reasons, what are the others?'

'At last, now you are talking. Master advised me to move out of town a long time ago. He knew that once involved in fight with goons, you will never get out of it. I ignored his thought.'

The moment he said something like this, I was shocked and scared. He looked at my trembling face and continued the reason.

'Trouble came from the local police man first, trying to use me for illegal things. I persisted to stay away from all this. Then he sent goons to convince me. I didn't know they are thugs, they behaved like normal people and talked to me nicely. They were clever enough to take to a place where they were doing illegal business. I sensed the danger and left that place without notifying. Then other gang who were opposite side of this gang got ready for a fight. I want to avoid involving in a fight with them and afraid they may drag me into something highly illegal.'

'You contacted Sekhar brother?' Trying to digest what he is saying.

'Yes. I had no other option. He took care of the inspector and chased those goons. Then they became violent and tried to attack me.'

'You had fights with them?'

'Yes, couple of times, before Sekhar arrested them. All those times I was afraid whether they might end hurting someone close to me. That's why I never talked about this to you guys and doesn't want to put you all in danger.'

'It is over now, isn't it?'

'Yes, for now. I am afraid some new gang will come after me if I stay here. Anjali is the only family I left with and I don't want her to be in any sort of trouble, especially because of me.'

'This is unexpected. Did you tell the same to your uncle and aunt?'

'Yes, I do trust them and felt better. Kept these things away from Anjali as it might scare her.'

'Yes, that's right. I thought one way or another I will convince you to skip the job and join school. After hearing these things, I can only say to go.' More in fear and shudder I wanted Abbay to go away for his own good.

Keerthi was coming towards us running and crying, breathing heavily, 'You are leaving town?'

Abbay stood up and said 'Yes, I am leaving. You know my dream to capture wild life, my dream became true.'

She hugged him tightly, 'how can I make you stay?'

Abbay kept his hands on her shoulder 'This what I want, remember I told you, my dream. It's not like I going to vanish tomorrow. I will come every year or six months once for at least couple of weeks.'

'You are one of my best friends. I will miss you for sure.' She was crying with hiccup. I was initially thinking she is doing too much. Now I too want to hug him. I knew Abbay won't like it, hence stayed back.

Abbay left for his job in couple of days. Anjali was crying till she came home from railway station. Suddenly the next day I felt like something is hallow in me. May be because from 2 and half years old few days has gone without him. I lost interest in the playing at the ground. Naren too isn't participating in the game.

There were no cell phones or SMS then. Our communication happened through land line as phone prize reduced. Every weekend Sunday he called to our land-line phone. I will cut the phone in a minute and call him back. The reason is we will speak for a minimum of 2 hours, this will make him lose lot of money. The major purpose for him to go for work is for his financial gains. If he is going to spend all his salary in call, all efforts will go in vain.

Couple of days left before new year commencement at school. To all our surprise and cheer, Keerthi's sponsor has sent her money for the term, bags, and books. She was very happy and thanked them. She also tried to give Abbay's money back to the family, but they suggest for some good clothes with that money.

Because of his absent, I too slowly begin to join in the *"Site seeing"* party. As per my knowledge flirting, blushing is good to health and it is a feeling due to chemical reactions inside the body. I began to think it is not wrong. I had a sizable number fan following as well, mainly because of my marks, I guess.

Suddenly dressing became key part. Hair style, walk, body language, even my throat and pitch changed. So far, no make-up or style. Now I spend lot of money in cosmetics like shampoo, different bathing soaps, suns screen, hair gel and fresh style pants no more regular fits; slim fits, low hip, and many others.

My changes were all visible to my family members. Only Aryan was opposing my drastic turnover and teased whenever possible. Mom and dad having gone through all these things before, only smiled when I did some silly things for style.

At school, there is a royal welcome for me. Except for one person, Keerthi. I was thinking she has ego problem and doesn't like anyone else getting praised other than her. She will warn me when I speak with girls. When I flirt with them, she acted violently at times and I was thinking Nancy's ghost is having effect on her.

We are grownups now and no more beating. There were punishments given occasionally for some students in the class. Overall, we got better treatment. If something goes extreme, they called student's parents and reported. This will end up in declaration letter from parents to accept detentions of students (*mostly temporary suspension*) and more than two detention means termination.

Abbay came back after ten months. He bought a gift for everyone including my mom and dad. We all went for game of cricket and enjoyed a lot. Abbay as captain still was very good. But his bowling, batting, and fielding was way below under the par. Lack of practise was visible. It lasted only for few days, then he was back to his best and dominated the rest of the matches.

Chapter 20 – Worse to Worst

One of the ugly moments happened was for Naren. Next street boys were teasing him for sometimes. Nirmal came to know about this and got himself involved in a fight. He asked for Abbay's help many times to crush those guys for abusing Naren. Abbay tried his level best to explain him and make him understand fighting will only make things worse.

Keerthi, my mom and dad, everyone advised Nirmal to control his impulsiveness. He lost hope when Abbay was stubborn to avoid fight. I guess he vexed because of Abbay's boring long philosophies.

Nirmal's fight with those boys made those guys to seek revenge. One day when Naren was returning to home, they caught him in the corner of the street and broke his left hand.

Nirmal was furious and was seeking vengeance. His dad slapped him and made sure he remains silent. Their parents want to end this. Nirmal unable to withstand seeing his twin's pain and plead Abbay to teach those guys a lesson. He provoked Abbay on various occasion talking about true friendship and care indirectly.

Exams were going to start and one afternoon dad was furious. He was talking and scolding Abbay to Anjali. She tried to defend Abbay's actions, but when mom too joined the party to take dig at him, without any choice she remained silent and left home. For Anjali, his brother is her known God. Talk non-sense about him, whoever you maybe, she will never talk or mingle with you again.

I am totally unaware of what happened, why dad and mom blaming him unnecessarily? I kept my head down and was getting ready to go to ground. Dad yelled 'You are going to meet that monster, right? No more friendship with that monster. Stay at home.'

I acted like I didn't hear him. Took bat and ball, went near the door and turned around 'I can say for sure you are wrong about Abbay. I knew him for the past thirteen years and he never done a wrong thing. If he had hurt someone, it will to be to save some innocent. I think you are over reacting, guess your BP is getting higher day by day. You must start jogging as he suggested for good health and stress-free life.'

I was sure what might have happened and pointed out directly that my dad is wrong. Dad was in shock to hear these words from me. He looked at mom in total disbelief. I went towards the door and jogged towards the ground.

Abbay was sitting alone under the tree. He might have gone and beat those Elangovan Street boys for Nirmal. 'So, you beat those Elangovan Street boys?'

'Yes.' Abbay slowly nodded his head.

'Nirmal provoked and you gave into the trap?' I was spinning the ball.

'Yes, provoked, demanded, irritated and forced me.'

'Looks like you have more enemies and less friends after that brawl.'

'I am glad that you came. I was thinking you too will be restricted at home.'

'Dad was saying few terrible things about you. I asked him to jog daily and reduce BP.'

We both laughed and when we looked up Naren was coming towards us still his hand covered and stitches on fore head was visible.

He sat in the middle of us. 'Why on earth you gave into Nirmal's trap? What's the need to do it on impulse? You knew why he was doing all those things, yet you are uncontrollable?'

'Yes, I wasn't as good in controlling myself as I thought I was. Your brother won.'

'Bull shit! Don't sell me the same crap. I know you better, why did you beat them?'

Naren's serious question shocked me and I was curious to know what Abbay will say. Abbay chuckled and as usual kept his hands over Naren's shoulder.

'These guys were doing dreadful things. Your brother was saying lot of things about them. I thought he was only blabbing to provoke me for fight. Then some of the things he told on them being womanizer, gangster kind of added to the things happening around.'

'That 8th standard student who committed suicide due to harassment?'

'I don't think a 13-year-old boy will commit suicide for harassment. I was actually supposed catch them one day prior.'

'You complained about them?'

'No. The police raided them and warned, but they were unable to find any proof and link to a big gang. One constable tried to follow them and they beat him to death. This innocent boy was trapped and set up by those guys.'

'Police had all the cases, eve-teasing, innocent beaten and everything. There was no compelling evidence and hence unable to do anything.' He passed for a moment and his head went down.

'Sekhar brother sought my help. I ignored him, though I owe him for saving me the last time around. I tried my level best to not get involved in any of these things. Sekhar asked to just take this one up and bring them down. If they were down for couple of weeks, police might be able to capture the entire underground mafia. I was reluctant and avoided it.'

Naren got the idea and narrated the rest of the story, 'Then the little boy died and Nirmal said he is dead because of you. I am sure he might have used your own punch lines against you *Having the ability to stop injustice and not doing so is also considered as crime.* Then you felt guilty and decided to yid police.'

Abbay continued, 'Well, you are almost there. He said many such lives will go and I am responsible for all. I decided it is the right thing to do. Informed police and couple of constables came with me in mufti.'

He took a deep breath. Naren confirmed 'You did beat those guys in front of Nirmal to ensure it was only an emotional outburst.'

'That's was their plan. I unleashed all my anger on them. They had good enough muscles, else would have been dead. It took 30 seconds max, for me to take those 6 guys down. Broke their legs, hands, jaws, face, and other lot of bones. I think Nirmal peed on his pants on seeing that.'

'Yes, I too think he did. He seemed petrified when he reached home. Mom and dad both hit him and told us to never see you again. Next year we will be shifting to some other town, I guess. Thanks to you!' Naren in a depressed tone.

'Sorry, buddy. I can't live up with the fact that, had I agreed and took those guys little earlier, a 13-year-old innocent boy might have lived.'

'I understand, I know you better than they do. How you are going handle Anjali and others?'

'Uncle and aunt know everything from beginning. In fact, uncle felt it is better to support Sekhar brother. Anjali...... will convince her in other ways. Other colony members don't want me around here.'

'What about those guys, any police complaint or violence case on you?'

'No, Sekhar brother's men took care of that. They are going to be behind the bars, in a crippled state or executed or encountered. Sekhar brother assured I will be free from any trouble as they have convincing evidence now.'

'You still trust police, after all you went through?' Naren put forward an important question.

'I trust Sekhar brother' Abbay finished off in a crisp answer.

'And the police didn't have any other option or choice except you to catch *"The big underworld mafia"*?' The same thought I was having on my mind. Naren really getting into the skin of Abbay now.

'They would have done it without me. After gym fight, policeman wanted to investigate us and processed to court. Sekhar bother sought us out of it by ensuring higher ranked officers that I will be useful for them in future cases.'

'Brilliant. You have been used like a paid mercenary.' Naren expressing his displeasure and prepared to leave.

'Guess you don't owe anyone anymore. Ok, buddy. Take care, catch you later' He greeted us and went along.

I threw the ball towards Abbay and he bowled with it.

'You know, I was right about you when dad scolded you. You did save many innocent lives by taking on the bad guys. You are a hero!'

'I don't want be one. I want to lead a normal life, enjoy and have an adventure each day.'

'Don't think it's in your cup.' We both chuckled.

'I lost three of my friends today.'

'Three? I know Naren and Nirmal. Who is the third? I am still here!'

'Keerthi was there when Nirmal was provoking me. She tried to stop Nirmal first and then me. She plead me to control it and I pushed her, moved forward. Finally, she said if I go now our friendship will be lost for ever and she will never speak with me.'

'Why she is getting involved in these things? What was the need to do this?'

'She was just trying to express her care for me. She thought I might stop to hold on friendship and I failed her. She is the one who is more upset and worried than me. Her argument and point of view is also right and practical;

by involving in fights, I am endangering my family and friends. It is 100 % right and true.'

'Hey, you did the right thing. One day she will understand that and speak with you. Until that day, knowing her stubbornness, she will evade you.'

'Yes, I know that. I am worried, not much. Have lost so many things, now I have better experience in leaving things behind. All close and loved ones will leave us at some point. We just have to keep on moving.'

'That was sad and boring, you can sure do better than that.' Few silent moments paused by after some laughter.

I want to change his grim face, so decided to tease him. 'So, you lost your only girl friend?'

'If you mean a friend who is girl, then I had lost one. I have many others.'

'Who? The old lady cleaning the drainage?' chortled.

'Yes, she too in the list. My cousin sisters....'

'Wait! Wait! They are your sisters not friends.'

'In that case, Keerthi is also my sister' Abbay is not allowing me to pitch him.

'All are your sisters? Even Vasundara?'

'No, she is.... or was a friend.'

'By chance, after school you communicated through letter or phone.' I was eager to know about them.

'She told she will write, but never got any letters from her.' Abbay tone indicated disappointment.

'Sometimes, you should take the step forward, buddy. You need my lessons on it.'

He chuckled. 'Everyone looks at me differently now, I think they afraid of me. I am happy that I saved someone's life by thrashing those criminals.'

'All due to our strength and ability to fight.'

'Yes, once you got into fight, it keeps on following till death in one way or another. If you learn fighting to defend yourself, people want you to hurt someone and have fun of it.'

'You regret your decision to learn fighting?'

'I will never regret any of my decisions. But I do agree I was wrong. This world won't let you live in peace if you decide to fight.'

'You unhappy, the way Nirmal provoked you?'

'Yes. He was putting demands and forcing his friend to do something that he is not willing to do. I felt that's wrong. Thirteen years together and questioning whether my friendship is true or false made me feel worse. He lost trust on me and I lost on him. In any relationship it is very important to trust each other.'

'As we grow older problems are creeping up'

'Yes, I was thinking last year was the worst year in my life. It seems it is going to go uglier and much worse moving forward.'

'We need to define worst, I guess.' We both chuckled and moved on to play the game.

Everyone in the colony afraid of Abbay. Anjali is not coming to our home anymore and she openly avoided Keerthi. Keerthi worried with her behaviour. She cried a lot one day resting on my shoulder. Things didn't improve anywhere. As everyone questioned about Abbay, now Anjali asking about her brother to me and few others.

Next week, the news came in paper about the arrest of the guys Abbay beat. Abbay thought it might calm his sister and her doubt on him will vanish. Unfortunately, it made her to fear her brother.

Though Anjali didn't express it fully, she is now keeping a little distance from her most loved and cared brother. Keerthi consoled her and both were spending time as before. My mom went to her home and checked with her, why she isn't coming to our home. Anjali accepted to come to our home, only after seeing Abbay nod his head. She is still very much her brother's girl. She won't be little baby girl at brother's arms for long time.

Abbay got next assignment and he is going to foreign forest lands of Africa and Brazil. He was very happy as his pay will increase because of abroad travel. One good thing happened in this year for him, I guess. He will come after twelve months.

Anjali was crying and keeping hold of him, proving how little, she knows about outside world and how much she knows beyond her brother. Keerthi, my mom and dad, Abbay's uncle/aunt, her cousin sister all calmed her down.

Chapter 21 – Only Try

The most important year of our career came. That's what everyone told us. I have been hearing for a while this tag line from many people for sometimes now. When we were studying in 10th standard everyone said the same. Now, we are in 12th standard and to get into good colleges this is the most vital part of our career.

I was sure to do medicine. The higher marks will decide how good a college I will get. Dad was very helpful in encouraging me and giving me various study materials that might help in exams. Though he wanted to become an engineer initially, as soon as I told my ambition to become a neurologist, he completely supported me in all ways.

One of the key elements in getting into the finest of medical institutions in our country is to get good marks in medical entrance examination which is separate from public SSC exams syllabus that we study in 12th standard. Dad wanted me to crack that exam and study in number 1 ranked college in India. I was really getting irritated of this craziness with number one rank. I guess it's by human nature.

Mom wanted me stay here in town and study in medical college in our town. It's second ranked within our state at that time. She was against the thought of going to some other state, staying in hostel, and struggling. She is a protective mother of course, even now.

For first couple of months, the entrance exams books and sample questions were interesting to me, but then I was struggling to manage school and entrance. Together doing both requires me to sacrifice play, exercise, and any other entertainment activities.

I was about to stop with entrance and concentrate on school exam. But, getting a great score allows me study in a great institution and get scholarships. I am little confused.

I missed my friend the most during this period. Any trouble I was having in making decision always a chat with him showed me the way, though his punch lines were inscrutable. I tried my level best though to contact from his office. Never got any response.

Around Diwali festival time, Keerthi came into our house with an amazing dress and makeup. Everyone in the colony pleased to see her smiling and happy. I am little concerned about her spending money unnecessary. Thought of scolding straight way, then remembered my best friend and what he would have done.

Only me and Keerthi was in the hall and watching TV. She softly asked, 'How do I look?'

The question looked very odd for me. We boys buy fancy stuffs, wear it, but never asked such question to anyone. I know girls do. Mom used to ask our opinion on dress or colour many times from childhood. This is the first time Keerthi is asking, I moved, wobbled bit and in a very pathetic position replied her.

'You, look great. Stunning! Great to see you happy like this'

She was exuberant. 'My sponsor sent a huge sum of money to everyone at home as they got great profit plus Diwali bonus. He/she specially gave 10,000 rupees for me.'

I was less enthusiastic compared to her. I was thinking why did she wasted all her money on a silly dress. Didn't have the heart to spoil her happiest day in life.

'Wow, amazing! That's a huge amount. How did you spend it?' The anger inside me got the better of me. I knew, it was a wrong way to put the last question to her.

She was still smiling at me unknowing the intention of my question. 'Well, I bought couple of dresses, books and bags. Then bought various thinks for all members at home for 5,000. Kept 2,000 rupees as saving just in case of any emergency. Now I have a bank account on my name.'

I wanted to slap myself. As Abbay says Keerthi is very good by heart and a wonderful person. Because of her situation at times to hide her vulnerability acts little harsh. My mind is full of negative thoughts. I was very ashamed and was only thinking how bad it might have gone if I had yelled or scolded her. Thanked my friend – saint, for his great punch lines and philosophies for a moment and looked at her with a smile.

'Even at your position you are trying to make others happy. You are truly wonderful and inspiration to us.'

Her smiled depth increased by an inch. 'Thank you! And you are an inspiration for me in many ways.' We chuckled and continued watching TV.

It always feels nice to have a nice little conversation with your loved ones. My respect for her went up from that day.

Studies are the only thing that matter for most time. Had to reduce my time at ground and exercise. I was doing exercise only on alternative days. Exams seemed to be very easy for me and I was sure to crack the most wanted "*Number 1*" again.

My entrance examination schedule is exactly a month from SSC exams. The complete confidence and satisfaction that I used to get before exams was missing. Dad sat with me for lengthy conversation about it. I was telling him, will give a try. He is a huge fan of Star Wars series and master Yoda. He will tell his punch line "*Do it or Don't!*"

The thought of quitting the entrance examination was going through my mind. Keerthi was 100 percent confident that I will crack it ease. I need some clear mind and luckily got call from Abbay and he is going to come in a couple of days.

I was eagerly waiting for his arrival. He came with three big baggage. He has bought something for everyone dear to him, including Keerthi. He tried to talk to her, but she ignored him. I became the commuter and gave her Abbay's present a complete set of foreign authors books on human anatomy and a beautiful wrist watch. She tried her level best to avoid it, in the end convinced her.

I got some sets of books on neurology and sports shoe, which I still have with me. He has given some gifts before on my birthdays, this was different as it was a foreign return gift. From the moment I saw him, wanted to have conversation on entrance exam. For three days Anjali and his cousin sisters occupied him. Finally, he came out and we headed to our usual place, under the big tree in Sphere ground.

'That's a lot of gifts you got there. How was the trip? Did you put on some weight?' I was trying to have an ice breaker.

'Put on some muscles. These wild forests were tougher than I expected and animals were unpredictable.' He took a deep breath already, very early!

'Adventure everyday trying to survive?'

'Yes, I really enjoyed. I am the best friend for many wild creatures now. Important one though should be "*Amol*" and "*Shealy*" lion and lioness. Amol really likes my company.'

I looked stunned and petrified by what he is saying. I knew this would happen. 'Great! Hope some tried to kill you and you had to fight with them.'

'Yes, fighting with those creatures was challenging. In fact, couple of times I lost initially with pack of wolfs, lions and elephants. I was running for my life many times. Then, slowly settled down, thanks to those tribal. Began to fight and win. They were on the run. Slowly, from tribal people learnt how to handle them and make friends. It was a wonderful experience.'

We both chuckled and after a couple of silent moments, 'I am really confused on taking the medical entrance examinations.'

'What's the confusion? It is must to get seats in top government institutions. I think you must take it. am I wrong?'

'You are absolutely right. I am little under prepared for this. I may pass it, but getting good marks is going to be a mountain climb. I am afraid slipping down is inevitable.'

'I have confidence in you. Twenty more days to go, put full effort in it, work hard and hope for the best.'

'I was thinking like that initially. But, conversation with mom and dad changed my thoughts. Dad in specific. Mom wanted to quit the entrance exam, because she doesn't want me to clear and go somewhere else. Dad saying too much things for my liking. He is saying old Yoda's tag line "*there is no try. Do it or don't.*"' We both are laughing looking at each other for some time.

'Star war's Jedi master "*Yoda*"? You guys tell me that I am cinematic?'

'Guess you kind of spread your charm to everyone near you.'

'Ha, Ha! You are neither a Jedi nor Luke. You dad is a simple human being and not master Yoda. Both you don't have any knowledge about the force. As a human being we can't see the future and we do not know whether we will be able to do it or not. We can only try. So, try it. It's better to lose trying harder than not even participating.'

'Wow!! Baba.... You are truly amazing. What a tag line! Can you please repeat it for me?'

'What, now you are going to memorise and tell the same to your dad?'

'Absolutely, yes.' I was hundred percent confident that dad will have no response for that. He repeated the lines and I memorised it. I was thinking all the way back to home, why can't I think of this?

As anticipated, when we were having dinner dad asked about my decision and when tried to reply, he threw the punch line. I gave him the memorised punch line and prepared for any counter arguments. Dad has no words to tell and acted like his concentration moved towards food. Mom raised her eyebrow and gave a sharp anger look at him, indicating his tag line ended in grave.

There was an unusual amount of confidence running through those preparation days. I was studying without looking at time. Abbay spent most of time at home, because the colony members are treating him little differently. I was at my home mostly with books, forgot to spend much time with him.

Entrance exams came, once again it sounded very easy for me. After the exams were over, I was very confident of getting good marks. Keerthi also felt it was easier than expected. From the next day of exam, almost 14 hours of day went along with my best friend. Keerthi was still ignoring him and he has decided not to engage with her anymore.

I found in a tricky situation with both friends. Many times, it was uncomfortable when both were around me. Abbay came to my home only once to give the gifts to everyone in my family, they took with less enthusiasm.

One night around 8 PM, electricity was not there in the entire colony. when I was going to have my dinner, heard a big scream. I heard this scream before. It should be Nancy, but why it was louder and it sounded different under no lights, it bothered me.

We all went out, just like others in the neighbourhood. Nancy was sitting with her hands closing the ears and eyes shut. Her father was trying to enquiry her what happened. Abbay was standing next to them.

Nancy was crying and unable to speak. Abbay's aunt gave her water and she slowly got up. Her dad again questioned, 'What happened to you, stupid girl? Why did you scream like this? Today is neither full moon nor new moon, then it can't be a demon.' He said in very high volume with same pitch.

'I was....... coming along...... in dark...... and suddenly....' Nancy was shivering and her words were shaking.

Her dad yelled at her again. 'What? What are you murmuring, you fool? Speak louder and clear.'

His statement made everyone angry and Abbay was furious, the way he is behaving with his scared little girl.

'I was coming in the dark and suddenly someone grabbed me and touched all over my body.' She was still shaking, but she must deliver now properly. Else, only thrashing will come from her father.

Her father looked around the mob. 'Who is that rascal? I will kill him.' He was folding his fingers ready to beat someone. Others got irritated and some moved backwards.

He suddenly stopped and looking at Abbay fiercely. 'Hey, boy you came before me here. You.... fighting bastard, you did this...?'

The hell broke and all looked shocked. Abbay was utterly furious and he is not going to keep silent after that, 'Hello, uncle. Mind your words. Like everyone, I came here after hearing the scream. Your son and security guards arrived before me.'

Abbay's uncle and aunt also chipped in quickly chorus, 'mind your words. You are the one who beat your own child mercilessly. You might have done it by yourself to scare her and make profit out of it.'

'You...' He is thinking about beating Abbay. But, he doesn't the guts to take Abbay. He turned towards his daughter 'Hey, you mental. Tell who was that?'

Shaken by the sound of her father yell, she said 'don't...... I don't know dad. It may the new powerful demon's son.'

Some of the people surrounding laughed. Her dad busted out in anger 'You mental. No brainer. Demon's son? You are the demon daughter.' On saying this, he came to thrash her. Nancy's mom grabbed her and pulled behind her. Because many people were watching, her dad has less option and he backed off. All people surrounding them cleared the area slowly, gossiping about the incident.

We all knew how bad they treated Nancy. It is rumoured that Nancy's father was the reason for her state. He only to get financial benefits, made false claims on his own daughter, when she was very little and made her believe she possessed with a demon. Couple of members in the colony filed police complaint against him for domestic violence. But they didn't last long as there were no proof. Nancy and her family members will support her dad and hence no chance of a success.

Chapter 22 – Dagger in the Heart

The next week Abbay got another assignment for project within India. Now, he is the official cameraman for the shoot. He acted very oddly for the next couple of days and unlike him. He was very sad. The only time I had seen him like this was at his parent's death ceremony.

Next day at Sphere ground, he simply sat under the tree and silent. I am not playing cricket these days, because it didn't give me the same excitement as before.

'What happened? Why this grim face?' making sure to jump straight into the subject.

'Something very bad happened. Unable to get over it.' He was looking down in a very sad and mild tone.

'If my guess is correct, the only thing that can make you sit like is a fight with Anjali' I was giving my worst probable guess. I was hoping he would say it was a silly fight with her. To my big disbelief, he said some unimaginable things.

'Not a fight with Anjali. The things she said and the way she is behaving really hurt me.' Abbay with tears in his eyes trying his level best not to let it go.

'She behaved in a manner that hurt you?' I was more worried than confusion or shock.

'Yes. From the time I came here, she was maintaining a little distance from me. I thought it was because she is a grown-up girl and she likes privacy. Later from my cousin, came to know she fears me.'

'Anjali, scared of you?' I was unable believe what I am hearing.

He nodded his head. 'She fears me, because I fight and break people's bones. I sat with her and tried to talk out of her misunderstanding. I told all the truth hoping it will make her trust me again.'

'It back fired?' From his expression predicted the reality.

He again nodded his head acknowledging my judgement. 'It made her only to keep further distance from me. I understood our relation can never be the same again.'

Unable to tell or ask anything further, kept silence for a minute. Then got the point he was trying to make; he is very sad because of something she said.

If he has consoled himself from her behaviour sure something that she told had really hurt him very badly.

'You said "*things that she said…*" what about that?'

He is going to cry for sure. Instead, he closed his eyes for a minute. 'Couple of days before, at dinner time, everyone aunty, uncle, cousin sisters everyone tried to explain and make her understand. She was reluctant on her thought that I am bad person. She finally said the unthinkable that she is afraid I may misbehave with her with some cruel intentions.'

I am not able to hear what he is saying. What? Is this Anjali? No way. Even last year, because mom and dad scolded Abbay, she didn't come to our house at all. How can this happen, is it possible?

I kept my hands on his shoulder and he cried. 'She is saying, I am a goon, who beats other people for getting name and doing heroism. And all thugs are the same, womanizers. That's what I did to Nancy and it is my true face. She knew a classmate whose own brother tortured her physically. She is comparing me to that murderer.'

He wiped his tears. But it kept on coming. He knew he is in playground and can't show emotion here. He stood up and turned towards the tree to hide his face. I am still in shock of the first sentence, his second sentence made me feel terrible. I stood up next to him.

'She was my little wee-girl. I know her from the day she is born. In my wildest of worst dream, I never thought of all the people she will think of me like that. My body was shaking, I was shivering when I was listening to this. Unable to hear anymore came out of the house. It was like a dagger in the heart pierced through.'

'I am out of words, Abbay.' Tears were in my eyes too, somehow managed to control.

'She listens everything I say. Only me, mom and dad were her world before. She didn't go to restroom without me on first day at school. She sat only within my arms on the way to school. I was the most trusted person for her. Now, everything turned upside down. I really miss my mom and dad Today. I just want to lay my head on her lap and cry. If they were alive, I wouldn't have to see a day like this.'

He wiped his tears and looked at me. 'One day she will understand and cry a lot for whatever she is doing now. She is just a little girl entering her teenage.

What good she knows? She is just blabbing based on what others near her said. It was not her fault.' He nodded and shaken his head very fast. How quickly he could change his emotions and console himself was beyond my imagination.

'Shall I speak with her?' I wanted to do something about it. I was also afraid doing anything will turn out to be another big problem.

'Not now. Maybe sometimes in future after I left for work. She is not in a state of mind to listen or think.' His thought sounded reasonable to me.

'Hey, don't think too much about it. As you said, she is just a little girl, believing in whatever others say about you. Once, she becomes more mature she will understand and will feel sorry for everything she had done.'

'Yes, I hope so.' Abbay chuckled towards me trying to move. 'I need to do something to change my mood. Shall we play a game of cricket, only you and me?'

I thought that was the best idea considering the current dilemma. 'I will bring bat and ball.' I ran towards my home.

All the way along I was thinking how can Anjali change like this? Who is doing this to her? I was also thinking about the option with Keerthi, may be if Keerthi spoke with Anjali things might ease up. But, will she talk good things about Abbay to his sister? With all thoughts going on my mind, took bat and ball and came back to the ground.

We played for a while and left. Abbay's train was around midnight time and there was no fuss this time. Only his uncle and aunty were there to greet him that too only from home. No one went him for send-off.

After a week tried to talk with Keerthi about Abbay and Anjali. But Keerthi didn't give me chance and kept on accusing him for putting everyone close to him lives in danger. After a certain point left her angrily, irritated by her speech.

Exam results came and was in top 10 rank holder in SSC and in medical entrance exam. As per my mom's wish, joined in the local town institution itself. We had a huge celebration and I was preparing to talk with Anjali.

After barely a couple of minutes of talk, I realized it is impossible to talk her out. Hoped it is only temporary and moved on. She was telling more non-sense about Abbay. I can't believe she is the one speaking all those things about him.

Abbay came three months once and he bought something for Anjali every time. She will not open the gift and simply throw it in the dustbin. I can only imagine how it might be for him.

Chapter 23 – Romantic Guy

College life was full of fun. Now girls become integral part of our life. My college bus will come by 8 AM to our bus stop. I will be in the bus stop around 7.15 AM. Our biggest and most crucial time of half an hour will be this. It felt good for me and instead of thinking too much was enjoying with my new friends.

Keerthi behaving very oddly to me. Every time we meet, we will end up fighting. She black mailed me about my bus stop achievements to mom and dad. Since, I am a top ranked guy, smart, clever, fit, strong, and handsome (*yes, a bit too much*) I can talk to any girl and I really liked flirting more than ever.

It continued for a while until next time Abbay came. One conversation with him changed me again.

'What are you looking?' Abbay questioned me when we were at the ticket counter of the theatre.

'Nothing. Just looking at those beautiful girls and keeping my health intact.' Looking at the girls and expecting out of three, one will turn towards me.

'I hate this, you have changed.' He was clear and straight forward.

'Buddy, this is nature. Nothing wrong in this. Stop being a saint. Are you going to avoid girls? No love?'

'I will love someone, only one. I believe in the idea of marriage and will share all my feeling with her alone. Looking at other girls, seducing them for time pass is wrong.'

'I agree your theory. But till I find my soulmate, unimportant things are no harm to anyone.' I was still looking at them in style tucked both my hands in jeans.

'It is a harm for girls who speak with you, thinking you are in love with them.' He raised his voice a bit.

'Hey, you are in 80s bud. Move on, no girl will think like that nowadays.'

'I will show you some real facts in you tube. Then you will realize.'

'Ok, ok. Looking at them is no harm.' Trying to convince him or trying to avoid further scolding from him.

He looked at and said graciously 'If it was your mother or sister there will you be looking them like this? They are someone's daughter or sister or mother and the way you guys' look will make them feel uncomfortable, it does harm them.'

Keerthi almost tried to say the same thing, just I didn't get it then. Now, when he told something like this, struck on me. I thought about this for very long hours, comparing with science and human behaviour. Finally decided he is right and followed the same.

Nowadays Keerthi is back like old days, no more fighting. Assume she had a problem with the way I was behaving with girls. Anjali was stubborn in her thoughts and nothing changed.

A year passed by, one evening me and Abbay was sitting at our usual place. Keerthi came to us fuming.

She looked at Abbay and there was a little uncomfortable silence. 'You went with Swetha for Hollywood movie?' Keerthi fully furious. She has little eyes, thin eye brow, lean body, when she talks angrily to me by default I will start to laugh. Same happened.

'Yes, I went with her. What's your problem?' I raised my eye brows and expanded my big eyes. Abbay was about to leave. I took a hold of him.

'I will tell your mom.' She is shaking, tried to threaten me.

'Go and tell. With her permission only, I went. Not only Swetha, we were five members.' In all possible dominant way.

She kept her head down for a minute and murmured within her.

'What movie you guys went to see?' She was asking more question and I got irritated.

'I will go to any movie with anyone of my choice. What's your problem?' moved much closer to her and threatened her.

'I do have a problem and will enquire you.' She was shaking more than before.

'I don't have to answer you and I don't care if you have a problem with that.' I turned towards Abbay and he pretending to look at the match.

A silent moment passed by. 'If I ever saw you flirting or seducing with Swetha or any other girl, will kill you.' Suddenly she turned aggressive, grabbed my shirt collar.

'I.... Will go with her. If...your stomach burning, you only have some problem.' Now I was little bit on the back foot, trying to figure out what's happening.

'You "*Site see*" or flirt or blush only with me. If I came to know you are doing with any other.......' She tried to be angry and it was funny.

Abbay was looking at us curiously. She noticed that and left.

'She is really mad, that girl. Now I understand why you fight with her.' I was still in a very confused state of mind.

'Yes, she is really mad at you.' He is looking little differently at me.

'What?' I am thinking more now, what just she said and what he is trying to convey.

'You are the world's most romantic guy? You gave that title to yourself, right?' He absolutely had a point there I believe.

'No. I.... am.... very romantic' Now I am more confused than before trying to relate.

'Oh, yes. You idiot. She just proposed you and you are such a tube light, still trying to figure out why she is so possessive about you.' He went a couple of steps forward to pick the ball coming towards us.

For a moment only able to hear a bell ring sound in hears. Steadied and with lots of confusion, 'are you sure? She told that in anger and wasn't shy or .... You know it will be little difficult to convey your love to someone, this was easy.'

'You are expecting a poetic love letter from Keerthi?' He was looking with the most teasing smile till date.

'No. When did I spoke about love letter. I just saying...... it has to be different than what just happened.' Still, I am doing some permutations and combinations of the situation.

'You know I believe when two people are in love, you don't need to really say or describe feelings for each other, you both know it.' He came up with his one more tag line.

'So...... I should know. If I don't then ignore her. Sounds a bit odd.' I was still speaking with a gap between words. The words and pitch didn't quite sync up. Honestly, I do not know what I am saying.

'If you don't like her and doesn't have any feeling for her, you can simply avoid. She will come to know.' He is getting under my skin now.

'No, No. I like her and feel her. But......' I closed my eyes and bit my tongue.

He was looking at me and I slowly opened one eye. He was laughing and I closed my eyes again.

'Hmm.... Great! I wish she was here to know that from you.' He is teasing me now more than before.

Realized that I am a rat in a trap now, I suddenly ran towards home like a little kid. I went straight into my room. Sat on the cot for a second and took deep breaths. I have watched lot of guys propose and the time they take to make it a perfect proposal. Poetic love letters, straight forward proposals, expensive fancy proposal, blackmails, etc. This is very new and completely different.

I thought about it for long time couple of days, mostly stayed at my room. I decided this not love. She is just possessive because I am her childhood friend. It's incorrect to conclude the way Abbay told. Jumping into conclusions are never promising idea in this matter. I had seen many such cases, where friendship wrongly interpreted as love and both people suffer in the end. He might have only teased me. I decided to stop thinking on it anymore and move on.

Abbay got another foreign project and he is about to leave town. Anjali stayed at home and I went with him for send-off. He was very disappointed that his sister has gone out of his reach and he was quite right. I am not talking with Anjali as before. She came regularly to our home and spends a lot of time with my mom and dad.

The next week college began as usual. I went to bus stop around 7.55 AM and waiting for bus. Something was different and I can feel it. Turned around to my right side, Keerthi was coming with her friends. She was chatting and laughing as usual. I tried to think nothing is happening and only normal.

I wasn't exactly normal. Irrespective of my mind saying to look somewhere else, I was unable to take my eyes of her. The needle like lean girl was looking stunning for my eyes Today. I was starting to notice her beauty. The same ant eyes, that will be hard for me to conclude whether it is really there in her face was getting my attention. Twice in the last ten seconds she looked at me with those eyes. The cutest of look I have ever seen from any girl.

I am still looking at her and slowly other girls near her noticed it and informing her. She was trying to ignore them and laughing about something, still giving a sharp cute look every five seconds. I can feel so much of chemical reactions happening inside my body. I was scanning her from toe to head, a black simple footwear, a watch on left hand wrist, a yellow bangle on the right wrist, mixture of red-yellow colour tops and light grey bottom, Chudithar. A little red lip stick, some face screen, her hair combed properly and looked like an angel to me, though she was wearing nothing related to white.

My fellow college students came near me and pat on the shoulder. Only then I realized how stunned I was looking at Keerthi. I can feel my heart beat was raising, my hands started to shake a bit. On top of all, a huge loud horn sound of the bus brought me back to the living reality world. I was trying to look at her in bus, in class, literally everywhere I was looking for her. The funny thing was she will come wherever I am expecting, probably intentionally.

We were spending more time with each other. The length of our conversations increased. Apart from talking at college, college bus, on way to our home, we chat on mobile too. We both had a mobile and students SMS pack came to our help. We both took same plan, 10,000 SMS for six months. We will finish it barely in 60 days. I will recharge for her too, when my SMS pack expires.

I can't remember, what were we talking all the time. It felt good for both us and we continued. I never proposed her or asked for her hands on my knees. We just knew both are in deep love and care about each other. That's all mattered to us. We never went to movie or beach (*we don't have a beach in our town*) or shopping. We never talked about these things either, yet we enjoyed our time.

I don't remember her first kiss or when we hugged first time. It happened only after we engaged. At my home, in my family everyone knew something going between us. They never showed or acted differently. Lot of things were different with us. When we talk or sit together with family to watch TV, we would be still talking with eyes. No one, but only we know the meaning.

The long break for Abbay was 12 months so far. In the call after 9 months, he said he has extended for another 6 months. His reason was understandable. He is going to come here only for me. I knew the reality and happy with every week call in mobile.

In the meantime, I came to know a news from colony neighbours that Abbay helped Nancy and he is taking care of her. It came a quite a shocking surprise for me. I remembered twice when he was here and at call he tried to speak about Nancy, but I shut him and changed the topic. Decided to check with him on this week's call.

Around Sunday night 10PM when I was very busy chatting with my sweetheart, got the call from Abbay. My darling understandably said Good Night, knowing we will talk for a minimum of couple of hours.

'Hi, buddy. How was Balu? Did he recover?' Balu is big bear in the zoo and fan favourite for his childish acts.

'No. His days ended.' Abbay expressing his grief.

'Ohh.... Hey, did you talk with Nancy?' Jumped right into the main talking point without wasting any time.

'Now you ask? How many times I tried to talk about her, you always ignored. Now what happened?' He is unhappy that I ignored his chat on this topic.

'Ok, sorry. Only yesterday heard rumour that you helped her, hence checking.'

'She was left in a mental asylum by her parents. She received lashes, humiliated, and tortured there. I paid the amount for her and got her out of there. Then arranged passport and took her with me. She is in US now, strong and healthy studying physics.'

'That's very neat, buddy. You would have said in one sentence, it was very descriptive. How you found her? What happened to the demon? You paid for her trip to US? You are paying for her studies?' I wanted to know more details on what happened.

'We were trekking last year and found her in a mental asylum. She pleaded me to help her and I couldn't leave her there. I tried to convince her there was no such thing as demon. She though agreed, unable to come out of her childhood fear. So, I convinced her to believe in God and if as she believes her God exists then it is impossible for demon to hurt her. Even if it did, bear the pain and pray to God, he will definitely help you. It was hard for her to accept what I said. I gave more speeches on reality and how she can move on from his.'

'And she agreed as simple as that?' I know these advises will not have any impact on her.

'It took a month for me to partially convince her. Then forced her to do exercise and mediation. As she was in a new place, hostel with new friends, she never had to be alone anymore. I think loneliness was the main reason for her. She used talk with me every day for an hour and trusted me with her life.' He gave a pass.

'You talked with Nancy every day an hour and you talk with me only once in a week and sometimes once in a month?' Jealousy is still there inside me.

'Oh, no. Not again. Drink some water to settle your stomach burning.'

'And the US? Her Studies?' My eagerness to know the next detail never diminished.

'I have to leave for the documentary in Brazilian forests and can't leave her here. With the help of one of my colleagues arranged for her stay and study. The money that I saved for Anjali higher studies and marriage came in handy. Yes, I paid for her trip and I am paying for her studies. Enough? Any other details like what plane she left? Or her current address? Anything you need more?' He is exhausted and done talking about it.

'Ok, ok. Cool. Make sure you keep something for yourself too.' Trying to give an advice, but decided to move on and changed the topic.

'Is there any understanding going on between you and Nancy? I mean talking every day in mobile for an hour with a girl, who you hardly know. This is something very new from you.' I was trying to put as eloquently as possible; guess ruined it.

'You are unbelievable. There is nothing. She is my friend and like my sister too. She needed someone to lift her life and I did that. You still don't know the anything about romance. I feel pity for Keerthi, ending by with the worst romantic person in the world!' He was furious and I kept my mobile a little distance away from my ears.

He helped the girl because of whom he suffered indigestible pain from his sister. The thought went through me the whole night. Wow, what a man!

It was impossible to convince Nancy to remain normal, only God knows how he did that. Anything that he earns he is spending for others without holding/saving for his future.

Chapter 24 – The Unthinkable

Keerthi and our love came into talking point at my home. There was no real fuss and dad simply told marriage after completion of MBBS. There was no drama and it went smoother than I hoped for. Mom was very happy as Keerthi is going to be her daughter in law. They had a great chemistry like mother and daughter, so it made my life much easier.

Next year, one of the local retailers with huge political influence got his sight on Sphere ground. The people in the colony moved to court to get stay, arguing it is a public property. Knowing that the retailer will lose the case in court, he sent goons to threaten our people. Twice in couple of weeks police arrived at the right time to keep those goons at bay without doing anything.

The verdict was going to be with us and goons stopped coming to colony. It was only matter of time now. Abbay arrived and pleased for me and Keerthi. Anjali now was treating him little better and few chat was going between them. He always said that they can never be the same after what happened, but he still wants his sister back desperately.

The next day, the goons arrived at the ground unexpectedly and trying to get playing boys into a brawl. We came to know about this and all gathered near the ground. There were an army of goons one side and furious teenage boys on the other. Few elders came along the way and tried to speak logic with thugs to avoid any violence.

One of the persons, 7 feet tall and nearly 5 feet wide teased a teenage boy and he beat him. Both parties are about to start a war by now. The elders and one constable came to separate them. I was holding Aryan and staying back trying to avoid getting into the fight. I remember very well all things Abbay said about getting into fight and spoiling future. I was reluctant to leave, grabbed my brother and tried to get out of the mob.

The gang leader of the thugs warned us and threatened to break our bones right now. While we are about to leave, the 7 feet big bulldozer came right in front us. He was about to come at us and we prepared to run.

In came a thundering blow on his face, Abbay standing there at the other side furiously looking at the bulldozer. Everyone heard the punch enough and all activities came to stall. The constable who was trying to keep the goons at bay, suddenly told them to go and fight with Abbay.

One more guy with a knife in his hands, came at Abbay. Abbay grabbed the neck of that 6 feet hippopotamus with left hand and lifted him like a pup. He might have choked the hippopotamus's neck for barely 10 to 20 seconds, he almost stopped breathing. Abbay left him to the ground and looked right through the leader.

The 7 feet bulldozer's teeth were gone (*at least 5 of them*), nose was broker and we can see the facial bone and skull, skin looked like tired off. He finally falls down unconscious. The hippopotamus was unable to move and giving actions for some water.

Abbay folded his fingers and he had a fierce look on the leader. The gang leader almost peed on his pants looking at his fellow thugs. He noticed that everyone already cleared the path for Abbay to dance and thrash these goons. The constable is now forcing the big fellows to go and have a brawl with him.

The gang leader signalled to others to leave and shuddered fellow members ran away. Four guys stayed and took the two unluckily idiots who tried to come at Abbay. After couple of moments the whole mob scattered. Everyone knew Abbay helped police in previous case and he could have easily sought for their help again.

On our way back to home, 'you should have grabbed us and ran. One more fight? It might ruin you again' was conveying my opinion.

'They we will keep on coming at us, if you run. For these people this is the best option.'

'Hope you thought about the consequence.'

He nodded his head. 'Anjali will go back to zero level.'

Suddenly Aryan pitched in, 'Sorry, brother. Because of us you got into trouble. I know if it wasn't both us you wouldn't have beaten that big tanker guy.'

'Hey, nothing like that. He deserves it. I did that to keep other innocent people safe. It was necessary.' Abbay tried to change the topic. Me and Aryan both know; he beat them because that bulldozer tried to injure me.

We both went back to home. Mom, dad had a long discussion with me to limit my friendship with Abbay. I am terrified and unaware of how to keep limit in friendship. Are there any limits in friendship? I didn't understand what was Abbay's mistake in all this? Why are they blaming him? Both got severe scolding from me and assured them that I will remain and maintain friendship with him for ever.

Keerthi came to our home and she wanted to speak with me alone. I know what she was going to say, so avoided couple of times. But, after dinner she came to my room to speak.

'I know you don't want to hear this. You scolded mom and dad, sticking for your friend. But......' I looked at her very angrily. I was serious suggesting my intention. She was little afraid to go ahead and she slowly sat next to me.

'I have no interest in listening to any non-sense on my friend. You may switch sides and change your thoughts about him. I don't change and he is still very dear to me.'

'I know your friendship. But true friendship is taking care of each other. Not putting one into trouble.' By the time she finished this, I stood up fumingly.

'What is true friendship line? Stop copying lines from mom. He didn't put us in trouble, he saved us.'

'He is arrogant, egoistic and doesn't care about others. He only wants to do heroism and he will put everyone's life at risk. I care about and scared of you getting into trouble.' She initially yelled at me and finally reduced the volume almost pleading to me.

'He is better than anyone of us. He is neither arrogant nor egoistic. He doesn't want to fight, it's just *"Wrong man at the wrong place at the wrong time."* He will risk his life for others and unaware of putting others in jeopardy.' I yelled even more higher volume.

'If you are going to stay with him, then you have to reconsider us too' She was shaking and scared.

I understood she want me to make a choice. 'I knew him before you and all the great qualities that you say admire about me came from him. If it is up to the point, I got choose between you and him, I will always choose him without thinking for a second.' I went out of the home and marched towards park.

I know she didn't mean that, but couldn't control my anger. Abbay was sitting there on the park's bench with two little cute puppies swirling around him. Now I think they are his best company. We acknowledged each other and both sat on the bench.

'So, had an argument with mom and dad?' Abbay knowing what might have happened asked the question.

'And Keerthi. Just now yelled at her and came.' Very serious in my tone.

'Hope you choose me, in given option between her and me.' He was right and pin pointed perfectly.

'Yes, I did. She was demanding, proof for friendship just like Nirmal.' Clearly suggesting my displeasure with her.

There was a moment of silence and Abbay begun again. 'It's different. Think from her point of view.' He once again graciously put forth.

'No, Abbay. I don't think she is right to demand like that.'

'Yes, but you think she really meant that way? She can't lose you. She is just protective about you. A bit more than our mom. She has gone through too much in life. Parent's death, aunt's torture, kidney lost, staying at orphan home, every year hoping she will get money for her survival from her sponsor. Just put yourself in her shoes. Now you got someone you love the most and he loves you too, would you not say the same thing that she told you now?' He put the whole picture as eloquently as he always does.

I was thinking and took couple of deep breaths. 'I should have maintained my cool. Told her something that I should have told in impulsive.' Realizing the fact.

'That's fine. In any relation it is inevitable to have difference in opinion and fight. You just should forget it and continue to love each other. Now go back to her and speak with her softly.'

'Yes, I will.' Nodding my head, took one of the puppies.

'I mean go now. She might me crying and thinking all miserable things of losing you. Go back to her immediately.' He was forcing me and I realized the point.

Went to my room and Keerthi was sitting on the corner crying as he mentioned. We both decided not to talk about Abbay and she won't force me to do anything that I am uncomfortable doing. I spoke with her softly too and then we discussed on subconscious mind class that happened last week.

I would have lost Keerthi if it was not for him. It's little too much to say that, we might have simply mingled again as she was preparing to ask sorry as soon as I come back. Because of Abbay her tears and fears might have reduced.

Another trip for Abbay and I was the only one to send off. Anjali has secured very good marks and she is getting ready to study computer science engineering. Abbay took care of all the financial matters. But she kept her distance from her brother.

We are in final year of our medical course and it is going perfect for me. Our engagement in couple of months and Keerthi is very much excited than me. An unthinkable event happened.

Keerthi fell critically ill, the one remaining kidney starting to show up. We admitted her in the hospital and as a medical student we both knew - she requires a kidney transplantation. It was very difficult to find a donor. We used social media and other networks seeking help.

One night while was staying and looking after her. She woke up and crying. I tried my level best to motivate her and keep the faith. I still remember her words 'I don't want to die Akhil. I want to live with you, cherish life with you, want to have many of your kids, grow old with you and live for at least eighty years.' Unable to say anything I came out and cried at the restroom.

I needed Abbay more than ever in this situation, yesterday when I spoke with him, he said he will be going to climb a mountain today. It will be impossible to reach him. Trying to keep faith, was praying to God. Those moments were extremely painful and hard to rethink.

I assume God heard my prayer. Next day, she got a kidney donor and transplantation done on the same day. The operation was successful. The donor doesn't want to reveal his/her name and only information we got the person is healthy and ticking after donating the kidney.

One month passed by and Keerthi is now strictly following diet and exercise. It was strict orders for her to remain healthy. She has moved to our house now and engagement is only 15 days away.

We are reconstructing the house on the eve of our marriage. Abbay arrived four days before engagement as I forced him to do so.

One afternoon, we were coming inside the house near veranda. I just instructed one of the worked to hold the steel rod carefully. I went inside and Abbay stood outside speaking with Aryan. I changed my costume and was coming out of the door.

The steel rod suddenly fell and coming right towards my head. Abbay was very quick to spot that and pushed me and Aryan away. Keerthi and mom came out. They only saw Abbay pushing me and both were looking at him furiously. I realized the dilemma and about to say thanks.

Keerthi was impulsive and went towards Abbay and accused of being a trouble maker. I was quick to point out what happened and everything came back to normal. But, Abbay has already gone towards his home.

I was waiting for him a long time at the Sphere ground. He came around only by 6 PM and the ground is empty.

'Slept in the afternoon?' I was trying to have proper eye contact with him. He was looking down and nodded his head.

'So, this all became messy again?' I know he is going to come up with something based on today's events. He has already said to me that the reason he is coming here is for me and his uncle. He said there is nothing left in here other than sadness and pain.

'Yes, I hate this. I want to cherish each moment of my life. I am doing that, when I am with wild creatures trying to kill me. Out here nothing to cheer or enjoy. Only sorrow and pain. Each time I come here something goes bad around me. I guess you are right "*I am always at the wrong place at the wrong time*".' He looked at me and we both chuckled.

'Yes. All these years it keeps coming at you. I wish we were little children, only cares about playing and fun. This grown-up business only making us stressful.' Acknowledged and was trying to take the conversation in different direction.

He was thoughtful again, looking down. 'Practically, we can't be children for ever. Everyone must deal with grown-up problems. It's just that I got tangled and unable to come out of certain things.'

'You will figure out something. You always do.' Trying to motivate and move on from the unpleasant situation.

'I gave hours of thoughts and made a decision. I believe I should take this decision for the good of everyone around me.'

'Stop, right there. Whatever you have decided, I am sure it was impulsive and wrong. I can tell this from your expression and body language.' I interrupted him knowing he has decided something worse.

'No, buddy. I am confident my decision is right. I have been thinking about this for the past two years. This was not in a haste. I must disappear from here once and for ever to avoid any more trouble to anyone.'

I looked petrified by what he just said. In complete shock and unable to digest his decision, 'that's your worst decision till date...... It...... is not practical and its non-sense. You are really thinking stupid and terrible. You are idiotic. A fool...... to make such decisions. People who are coward, doesn't have the gut to face their problem only will take such a decision. All the philosophies, tag lines and punch lines you thrown at others, you should first consider them. You are a coward......... advise is only for others and you won't follow it. What happened to win-win scenario? Always there is a way?' I was furious, anger and frustrated. I know very well about my best friend; he is not going to blab or kid on these things. I wanted to scold him, hurt his ego, and make him reverse his decision. I am with full determination to talk him out of it.

He chortled at me, was expecting such outburst. 'I still believe there is a way out and this is it. I am unable to bear the way Anjali looks at me or talk to you. I do not like to describe it further as it the most uncomfortable scenario I came across. If I stay around here, fights will always follow me. People know I can fight and for money, power, pride and even for fun someone will always want to have dual with me. If I go away from them any other place in the world where my identity is unknown, I can be just a common man living in peace. Also, there is an option at jungle. I can make good friends over there as well.'

I was cautiously listening to each word coming from him. Again, interrupted his flow 'Did someone asked for fight for pride or fun?'

'Every time I come here, there will be some stranger or known person who what to flex their muscle against me. Goons, thugs, karate students, martial arts students, gangsters, etc. all want the same thing. All I ever did was fight for scholarship at school and then once fought to save innocent lives. It changed everything. There are many instances these people tried to hurt people around me, including you. Police, Sekhar brother helped me to take those guys out. Anjali is right to fear me and so is Keerthi, I do put my loved ones in danger after every brawl. I must somehow put an end to this. Only option I see is this.' He gave a pass and both were looking at each other in disarray.

'What if Anjali understands and you both became the same as before?' Looking for all kind of possibilities after his speech.

'I would have taken her with me. As I said, this place will haunt me one way or another. One more thing, it can never be the same between Anjali and me. Way too many things happened. Even she understands everything and make sense out of all, there will be always a little niggle deep inside. Even my parent's death didn't hurt me as it did when she thought I will do something to her. I will never get over that.' His eyes filled with tears ready to come out and so was mine.

'You said disappear? You are going to change identity?' Now I knew it is impossible to change his decision, I must look for other options like talking in phone and seeing him occasionally.

'Not immediately. Eventually I must change my identity to live in peace and avoid anyone getting hurt or put anyone in trouble. I am sure it is better that way.' Abbay got his tears under control and getting himself ready to ask me something. He stood up and walked towards the tree and I followed him.

'I had never asked anyone to make a promise that is going to benefit me. I am going to ask you now. Please......' I grabbed his shoulder, turned him towards me.

'You have already told enough things that I couldn't bear. Stop making it further worst.' Tears came out of my eyes.

'I have to. Sorry! Please promise me that you won't try to contact me or search for me ever in your life.' That's a nuclear blast right in centre of my heart. I was unable to react and speak or do anything. He continued.

'If we continued to talk on the phone or meet, one way or another I will put my loved and dear ones into trouble, knowingly or unknowingly. It is safe for everyone that we don't meet or talk again.' Abbay said with same pitch without a glitch. Throughout this conversation he was crisp, clear and spoke with absolute conviction.

'That's unfair on me, Abbay. I can't just let you walk off me for ever. I always need you.' Now tears were falling from both of our eyes. Both maintained the eye contact.

'No, Akhil. There is no other way out of it I believe.'

'What are you hiding? I know something big has happened to make this decision. Please tell me, you were there for me many things when I needed or had problem. Let me stand by your side and deal it together.' My mind stalled and desperately wanted to avoid the promise.

'I am unwilling to tell anything further. I have told enough things I shouldn't have told. I want you to understand, trust me and promise me.' He was sure and moved his hand towards me.

'I can't promise something that makes me not talking or seeing you forever.' I insisted.

'Ok, I will find you at some point in life. May be after 10 or 20 years, when everything settled down. But I want you to promise me that you won't come after me searching until that.' He was signalling to his hand.

'I trust you and I know at some point you will meet me again. I believe in your word. Just remember there is someone, who is waiting for your arrival. I regret your decision to learn fight, I wish your mom and dad were alive. I wish we stay friends together till the end of our life time.' More tears were coming and I kept my hand on his, promising for what he has asked me.

We both hugged very tightly. The tears were flowing like flooded river steaming and taking out everything on its way. Almost twenty years since we first meet, it is irresistible emotion coming out of us.

We both wiped our tears and moved towards my home. He left with a good bye. I recollected every occasion, every speech, every funny moment, sad occasions, his boring philosophies, things I learnt from him, things I might lost if it was not him, things I will miss in life without him. It was endless till the morning sun rise.

Abbay came to our home to say good bye to everyone. Everyone just acknowledged as if he is going to come back next year. Keerthi just spoke a word "bye" and left. He wasn't expecting much either. He hugged his uncle and aunt. They were crying and I realised that he told them too. Anjali gave her hand for an awkward hand shake and he acknowledge with tears in his eyes.

As usual, I went with him for spend off. We tried our level best not to cry, but in the end before train left, both hugged and cried. It was melodramatic when I think about all of it now, too much of emotions. Guess that what human means.

I had couple of sleepless nights and finally decided to move on and cherish my life with Keerthi. Always there was something missing. His uncle and aunt are not speaking to Anjali normally. She's sad to know they are behaving like this because the way she behaved with Abbay.

He was not there for my engagement and was missing him during my reception. I tried not to show it, Keerthi realized it. She asked me to call him, I knew he won't come. Tried anyway for her and was unable to reach. Keerthi tried desperately to reach him, so did Anjali. My marriage concluded without him.

Keerthi wanted her sponsor to be there for her marriage. After communication back and forth, she only got letter with blessing and best wishes. A gift, a nice doll with boy and girl sitting under tree. The blessing meant a lot to her.

Chapter 25 – The Reality

A year passed by and Anjali came to know Abbay left for ever. She came to realize all the things and it was way too late. She cried a lot with Keerthi.

Her uncle and aunt were not ready to forgive her and maintained distance. My wife and Anjali pleaded with me to help them in searching him. I told the truth what happened and my promise.

Abbay knew, I know him too much and if I come after him searching, I will find him out for sure. His promise was a clever thing to do.

Anjali started searching for her brother following the threads from his work place. She stuck at certain point and unable to proceed. She never gave up her hope and continued. She loved her brother way too much to let him go, but she was only to blame herself for everything that has happened.

Me and Keerthi had our first our child. We named our daughter *"Vasundara"* I wanted to keep this name in memory of my childhood friend. Couple of years went by and Keerthi now become a heart specialist. Heart surgery and lifesaving dream is not far away.

Keerthi is the best thing happened to me. She is lovable, takes care of me and loves me so much. We barely had any fights or differences or arguments. Both of us had a great understanding, know each other very well. My life was full of happiness and joy. Thanks to my amazing wife, without her I will be nothing.

Keerthi is now more serious in finding her sponsor and the person who donated her kidney. She was stubborn and felt she owes those two persons her life.

From the orphanage home the message is that, her sponsor wanted to give a letter and disclose his/her identity on Keerthi's 25th birthday. She respected their decision and waited for it.

Her kidney donor never wanted to find out. He/she has made sure of that in several ways. Keerthi was doing everything she possible can to find them.

Keerthi's 25th birthday came. She was eager to know the sponsor and running out of patience to read the letter. Everyone was there, Anjali, Abbay's uncle and aunt, his cousin sisters, Aryan and his girlfriend (*Yet to marry*), mom, dad and neighbours and Keerthi's couple of friends from orphanage home.

Her friends from home too wanted to know because, the same sponsor helped them a lot financially for their studies and survival. I got a call for emergency patient who met an accident. I rushed to the hospital.

I came back home around 5 PM, with a full satisfaction of saving a life. Perfect day so far from morning. Entered the house and there was an unusual silence. My home is not like this. Vasu should be awake by now, she is yet to speak, but if she is awake everyone should be around her and enjoying.

I opened the door and saw Aryan, dad and mom sitting on the sofa with a grim face. I know something went wrong. I was hoping for the best and without asking them anything tried to go into my room. I felt a huge surprise to see Anjali sitting next to them and wiping her tears.

That made me to think about lot of stuffs. Is there some shocking news on Abbay? Some terrible thoughts came into my mind. I didn't want to go to Anjali and talk anything. Rushed towards my room. Keerthi was crying and wiping her tears with letter in hand. My heart beat was rising and scared to death.

She gave the letter to me, still crying. It was the letter from her sponsor. For a moment there was a big relief for me seeing that cover, it may be even the nastiest news from sponsor, but my only thought was it was not about Abbay. Took a deep breath and slowly with little smile inside opened the letter and read.

It started like "My dear friend Keerthi," I was in full excitement wanted to read the rest of the letter. I wasn't thinking about anything else. Simply going the letter.

'If it was up to me, I would have never revealed who is your sponsor. But my dad promised you, once you became a doctor specialist in cardiac related things you should know it was him. I must keep his word. Yes, your sponsor was my dad. He was thinking about adapting you at first, then he was afraid of your aunt's legal implications and her threats. He found another way and sent you to orphanage home. Dad wanted to ask Sorry for that, please forgive us.

By the time your aunt was no more a threat and we were financially stronger, he decided to adapt you, some unexpected things happened hence unable to do so. I know lot of unpleasant things happened between us, forget them all. When I told dad that you want to repay us, he said, *"Instead of wasting time by thinking about repaying us, when she became doctor ask her to save a life in that minute."* I am going ask the same to you and I know will. You a wonderful girl, now women with amazing commendable qualities. Just be yourself. Cherish every moment of your life with my dear friend.

With love your sponsor's son,

Abbay.'

I was about thinking all the things happened in the past. I know how Keerthi might be feeling right now. Decided to calm her down. Folded the paper and looked at her, she was crying with extreme guilt. I know I must make her realize none of the things happened was her fault.

'This is definitely written by him. Look at that idiot's handwriting, inscriptions on the temple. One thing he never ever changed.' I chuckled and said, without knowing what to say further to change her thoughts.

She was still looking at my eyes. She stretched her hand to give another paper. It was a medical report. She used all her detective skills to find out the kidney donor.

'So, detective Keerthi succeeded! Two jackpots on the same day. Quite astonishing birthday presents you are having.' I got the letter and without knowing what's in there, was keeping a laughter.

The name in the sheet was "Abbay" and he has given his company address in Africa. I just closed my eyes for a moment. This bloody bugger has done it all.

Keerthi fell suddenly in the ground with a shock, I tried to grab her. She kept her head on my shoulders and started crying. She then hugged me tightly.

'He....... went to fight boxing for scholarships and sponsor for me to get new dresses and books. He went to part time job...... to pay my school term fees. When he wasn't doing any job....... I didn't get the term fees money. He went to forest and jungles fighting for his life daily, so that I could study medicine, buy new dresses and cosmetics. Even though I fought with him for silly things...... he kept on helping me morally and financially. I didn't even spoke with him and I was the reason for his split with his friend. Yet, he only protected me. Finally, gave his kidney to save my life. I didn't even say proper good bye to him, Akhil. I am the worst person on this world. I was cruel and only hurt him.'

'Look at me. None of this is your fault. He always thought you as sister and he will forever. He wrote this letter before he left. Look at what he said, "*a woman with amazing commendable qualities.*" He knows you better than all of us. Now, at least try to do what he says. Instead of wasting time crying for that idiot, save a life.' I was blabbering unable to find right words or correct tone. How can I console her? Wish he was here to help me out.

'We need to search him, Akhil. I need to plea and seek forgiveness for everything I done to him. Help me find him.' She is in a haste to find him.

'I make very less promises, I made one promise to my dearest friend. Whatever happens I keep that one. He named as "*Hallow man*" for a reason, you can find him only when he wants. He said that he will come and meet me, I am sure one day he will and I am going to wait for that day. You move on and cherish life with me, ok?'

I tried a lot to convince her. She cried and kept her grim face for a week. Instead of giving up, I opted for few more extraordinary ways to convince her. Dance, movie, restaurant, etc. nothing worked. I am terrible in romance, as Abbay said once.

After couple of weeks, she decided to search for "*The Saint Abbay*" along with her friend and his sister, Anjali. They searched for him very hard. Knowing he was in US, even we arranged a trip. I took this opportunity to have a good vacation. We came to know his last official name was "Suriyaputran"

I was laughing about the new name and joked to Anjali and Keerthi that there is possibility he might have even changed his face by plastic surgery. They took that seriously and went after plastic surgeons in US.

We turned back and a massive surprise came by means of Nancy. Form the television news we came to know that she is a nominee for Nobel for her unparalleled work in "*Black Holes and Event Horizon*" that's the first time I heard about the term "*Event Horizon*". After the interview she thanked her close friend and mentioned he is the person responsible for everything she has achieved and she always dedicates to him without mentioning his name.

We all know who she is talking about and the next moment Anjali and Keerthi were busy in contacting Nancy to get any information about Abbay. The approach quite back fired. They got nothing expect a photo of him attending Nancy's weeding. She now has two boys named as "Abbay" and "Suriya" both named after her close friend.

Couple years passed on and yet no idea for anyone. Neither Keerthi nor Anjali quit or stayed back. I was enjoying their searches with Anjali's fiancé, who is also a software engineer like her. He is a travel guy and we enjoyed each other's company. Sometimes Aryan and his wife joined us. We went various places, US, Brazil, South Africa, Egypt and even to Antarctica (*plenty of money and plenty of time wasted on this one as it was neither a travel place nor an enjoyable one*). Every 6 months we took off for a trip.

We welcomed our second child, a boy. Keerthi was adamant to keep his name, you know whom I was taking about. I tried my level best not to, failed. He is cute, loved by everyone and he was very muscular even as a little kid. The searching continued. Nancy came to our home and on a chat with her, she was telling some punches of our friend. When he said all those things we made fun of him, now everyone was listening.

One of the famous one she said was, "*The great Gods we worship in all religion were once human. Their amazing qualities and the way they treated and cared for all living beings made them worship like Gods. They possessed qualities and thinking that were one step ahead from normal human beings.*" Quite right as he always, made a lot of sense now.

Anjali expected a lot that her brother will arrive for her marriage and only got disappointed. She is now a mom of a boy, luckily the little boy got a different name, not his mom's brother name.

It has been four years, since everyone knew about Abbay. I used to wonder what it would be like if he never came in life. There are way too many things starting from crossing road alone as a kid, loving my brother, keeping my health, a wonderful wife, thinking in other's point of view, dealing with anything coming at me, etc. It's an endless list. I miss him.

I am sure, one day I will see him again. I want to have conversation with him, spend time and have fun. Awaiting his arrival eagerly.

This is Akhil, signing off in hope to meet "My Bad Friend!"

Acknowledgement

I believe that the most precious thing in this world should be something that's impossible to get back. Everything in the world has a cost and bought in some way, by money or gold or actions or speech. The one thing that doesn't have a quantitative value and impossible to buy back by anyone in this world is "*Time*"

Time, the most precious thing of all. Today the world is a busy and fast paced place, where there is no time, to eat or sleep or even say a "*Hai*" to our own blood relations. Thank you very much for spending your precious time in reading my writing.

Have a pleasant rest of the day!

Also by P G Seshagopal

My Bad Friend
Is It There?
Not My Mom Anymore
A Brief Look into Freshers' IT Job Interviews